A Window Opened

Alan Martin

A Window Opened

This book is written to provide information and motivation to readers. Its purpose is not to render any type of psychological, legal, or professional advice of any kind. The content is the sole opinion and expression of the author, and not necessarily that of the publisher.

Copyright © 2024 by Alan Martin.

Printed in the United States of America.

ISBN   978-1-64552-236-2   (Paperback)
ISBN   978-1-64552-235-5   (Digital)

Lettra Press books may be ordered through booksellers or by contacting:

Lettra Press LLC
30 N Gould St. Suite 4753
Sheridan, WY 82801
1 307-200-3414 | info@lettrapress.com
www.lettrapress.com

Pictures were inspired from record albums, thanks to
Mountain, Savoy Brown, James gang, and T Rex.
To my family and friends.

Contents

Section 1

Fantasies Seen in a Window

Between Realities

BEYOND THE TWILIGHT of the moon and stars, a glimmer of shadows dancing as foretold in the days of old were forming. As the sky turned into a crystal eclipse showing its dominance in power, it moved on its own accord.

Appearing its brilliant brightness to serve its own purpose as the shadow of delusion sparkled with its own destiny the presence was cold. In frost of its suspicion, the image of its existence was cataclysmic wondering if it would survive.

When it became more radiant and translucent, mere eyes could not look at it. I wondered with astonishment and was blinded by this disarray!

As my mind was preoccupied with confusion, I felt my conscious was losing its sanity! During the absence of my conscious, I found myself lying on the floor in a trance. I've seen visions through the ceilings and walls of the outside world.

Bewilderment and the unknown of my conscious caused confusion to circumvent and look at my subconscious. As I explored my subconscious, the reality of it showed my conscious was dismayed! I asked myself, "Why?"

Far above, the shadow swiftly moved across the horizon amongst the stars; it prevailed into darkness overwhelming the sky above. As the universe became black as coal, I saw no stars or light. I sat and wonder with curiosity as my mind became occupied of this unusual sight.

"Then I thought we were all doomed!"

At this point, I heard the roar of thunder, and lightning started to flash across the sky. I looked shaken from the sudden change; there seemed to be a war in the far heavens.

Could not actually see what was transpiring in the clouds above, but the brutal visions I observed, I thought to myself, "Am I going crazy or delirious?"

In this nightmare of sanity was there a relief of my mind or was I entering a place of no return? As I held on and the darkness subsided with the break of dawn, the brightness of the sun overshadowed the darkness that prevailed. "The trip was over for another day."

Twinkling of a Fantasy

Upon the twilight of a glowing light, a period before the darkness of night may show an elusive appearance that got away. From a vision, we observed a delightful image, which may not be restrained within our sight. The colors of glitter that stares at us from above may show an impressive display that one may not hold "like a twinkle in one's eye."

"A capricious impulse of your thoughts could be pleasing" like sleeping on a mountaintop of tall grass, dreaming of valleys full of exotic flowers beautifully arrange. Could the enjoyment of a twinkle inspire the gaiety that flashes when dancing like stars that sparkle along the edges of shores along the sea skies? An intimate moon flows with softness gliding itself across the horizon to show off its flare.

Has the illusion of sensation pass through an unsuspected mind or are we waiting for the next fantasy to visit us again?

The fantasy of dreams may come to be a source that has been stored, not quite understanding the dependence that it holds on you. This temptation of discourse could allow an obtrusive contemplation, not realizing the consequences that one may be subject to. Will the wandering mind look at this as a farce trying to find the comical side of this unusual dilemma?

"How does this shiny flash happen so fast" that in the brief moment, it appeared it was there, and now it's gone? Is there a way to keep your imagination intact or "has the image flew by and been swallowed up," not giving any response to ask if this is real or not?

Would this unawareness lead to a delirious onset, "being lodged within one's mind, and it feels it's stuck in a four-walled room, and you can't find your way out, but you keep looking for the door?"

"While staring across the rivers and fields of meadows, you seem to focus on the ceilings of glass, and you see approaching is a quarter moon smile, and your eyes sparkling like a star gazing in the winds of chime. You hear the bells ringing some sort of an enchanting melody."

"The twinkle has a tendency to sneak in and get a glimpse to see if it can catch you by surprise," allowing to show you this fantasy that put you in a persistent delusion, "not grasping what one knows or sees!"

Can one acquire the perception needed to avoid the imbalance that seems to pursue the imagination? Or has this unnatural instability remain within to become a misleading conception? "Did we happen to lose any fragment from our mind or are we following the fantasy that guides us to a carnival on the hill?"

Will pieces from a daydream show a desire to fulfill the glare, which took you by the hand and lead you to the clouds above, "so you could talk with the winds of time?" You find yourselves looking upon this wild visionary fancy with no comprehension of your where about, the twinkle shined, and it brought forth a gleam of brightness that glowed on your face.

This impressive sight seems to be above our normal heights. "Has a phantasm of make believe bring us an uncontrollable mindset, wondering is this all a dream? Thinking may come to bring us a conclusion that's unsubstantial amongst our sanity." Did this just become a typical formality that was engaged from years back? Or has there been a pattern set in an orderly fashion, and we did not recognize it?

"It appears as the fantasy walks upon the dust of the clouds, it's waiting for the twinkle to illuminate out of the dark!"

"Hearing the fluttering of wings gathering around in a circle 'to watch the fantasy crying from a floating mist of greenish smoke' as hands and arms were reaching out of the ground trying to reach the sky, and the twinkle flew by to bring joy to the light, amazed from its glow brought insight to those who know."

"Allowing the fantasy to flow alone looking for its own harmony while the twinkle keeps blinking as it rides a wave on a celestial star trying to find its way home."

"Will we not let the twinkle be content and welcome the fantasy when it shows up?"

Shadow Dancing in a Lamp

A SHADE OF flickering exposed a glow of movement running up and down the walls expressing a joy of action as if it was dancing.

This altercation showed different styles of rhythm flowing freely along the reflection of its light.

A flame burning and jumping around as if it was trying to talk to you hypnotized your view. As the crackling sound of its voice opened to make one watch the source of its sparkle, the fire and heat it possessed is charming but can be alarming.

This cloudy mystical image was flowing "like a ghost caught in a mirror!"

This unpredictable transition, changing its form and movement, was bouncing to a point which had you following and looking at this inquisitive sight. Your imagination was out on a limb "dreaming," not knowing what may come next.

Along with the oil burning wick held inside a glass tube, this ornament was proudly decorated with a stand. Understanding the brightness that it displayed intensified the heat of its splendor, and I found out it was too hot for me! But if we could "dance like the fire," we would never get burned.

After glancing at this rhythm, it formed a surprise announcement and staged a glare, performing spectacles that left you speechless. Crossing the halls of walls "enlighten the twinkling;" it was providing, illuminating even the faces of others.

Look out for the keenness along the edges, for they may be sharp enough to cut through and penetrate the darkness that surrounded the object within its eyesight.

This strange phenomenon overwhelmed a provincial behavior, staring continually at the obstacle that once was playing on the "strings of light."

Has this clairvoyant glitter shining its radiance flaunted itself, instructing those around to guide themselves?

A passionate style of rhythm was kissing the edges of the tube as it was wiggling along the borders of the glass. This shadow was hugging the tube, and it didn't want to let go, dancing freely up the invisible glass and heading for the ceiling. Each time it would leave, another shadow took its place.

"A vibrant shadow" swinging back and forth, running as if it was a pendulum, brings attention, noticing steam and mist drifting in the rafters, longing for the attic along the roofline.

Could this "gloominess dance" outside the glass container it was trapped in? I was witnessing a bewildered sensation that increased my stimulation.

This peculiar dilemma has me concerned appealing to my own sanity. Was I seeing a fragment of my imagination watching a foggy breath of air circling around entertaining a mirage of smoke?

The light in the lamp brought another shadow into play; now the dance has started again. While watching the "glow of the light," the shadow moved slower than usual.

I wonder if that was caused by a slow and dim-burning light? Or was it just grooving with the flo…ow…oh no, no, no, it's getting low on fuel; the oil is spent.

The twinkle that once glittered went out; the evaporation smothered the "dance in the lamp."

The Light from Yesterday

"Oh, I see hands. I see ten strange faces" reaching out to send us a helping hand from the mountaintop with "ten sticks of shiny lights!"

"I've seen years" of precious time wasted with answers unknown, "saying please" send us a helping hand.

"I hear the thunder with its crushing heart crying!"

Showing a sparkle of the stars twinkling and the moon glowing, "I have seen shadows" romancing along the "lights that was inquired from yesterdays."

As the night flowed along the sky of time, "I noticed the glitter that twinkle," expressing the "twitter that shined."

With a beam of its brightness showed its flashes as a spark that ignited the "clouds with laughter."

This lightning rod sent streaks of "light across the horizon." Showing its dominance in power, it crossed the open realm that was in sight.

Nothing in its way affected the course of its path; this source of radiance has a direction whether coming or going. While looking upon, you couldn't see with the "lustrous sheen of its glow!"

Who would be able to stand in the way of its clear reflective luminance as "fire was showing its rays beyond glory?"

Have you ever seen the "spark of an arc," where the light shines so bright that your eyes could be looking at the sun directly, and you find yourselves seeing yellow spots?

As the matter was unoccupied allowing the mind to become unbalanced, forming delusions that was misunderstood, you drop your hands from your faces to try to find the equation!

This slight dilemma of confusion caused me to see things beyond the ordinary sight and look pass the days of tomorrow.

Far above amongst the stars, this course of light brought some sight "showing the brilliance of its might." With "spectrums floating by with colors of the seventh kind," my wonderment had me in suspense of what I may see next, for this illusion I'll never forget!

As I gander toward the heavens above and the sky was as clear as water on a reef, I pondered watching the sparkles that formed on the surfaces.

This deceptive image had me fooled; the clouds of disruption came in; and the winds of time came forth to move the ocean tops, so it may regain its course.

My mind had lost hope for a minute or two being mistaken of its identity, for this illusive form was already gone!

As the galaxies belong to the stars of light shining with brilliant brightness and surrounded by the deepest darkness, the "crystallize gem" seems to prevail itself across the emptiness.

In a space above, this transparent diamond sparkling this attractive glaze seems to catch "one's eye!"

"While glancing, the glare of a gleaming light struck me" as it seemed to stare pondering its "vision in my sight!"

Had me wondering what is this, for I started to "fear her shiny light on me," and it must have known?

"Sharing an eye-to-eye" contact upon studying each other's observance startled my surprise of what may come.

This unusual curiosity within one another had me strangely examining my thoughts of what just happened.

After finding myself in a disarray state of unbelief, I questioned my integrity, asking, "Did we see this or not? Or have you been staring at the sky to long?"

There was a fleeting appearance that flew by in which we caught a glimpse of something that "twinkle a sign to me three times. I looked and asked myself why."

"Is this a dreamed-up hypnosis or was it a proposition?"

A feeling was sensed by this exquisite sight; "a guidance of light" came along to remind me there will be an engagement that you will see.

As you looked toward the mountain peak, "there stands a woman shining her brightness." I wondered, "Is she all right as we stood there from a distance?"

Then we asked, "Who is she?"

A voice replied, "The queen of the light! She is the one who gave you a twinkle thrice!"

With her sparkle, she smiled, and suddenly she flashed away leaving a goodbye.

"I never saw her again except in the sky."

Standing with the Clouds of Rain

ALONG THE FIELDS of stubble and high grass beside the roads of slush, the guise of singleness enters and stands with a stagnated stale. This flagrant staunch surpasses a becoming stench, which allows it to erode amongst the clothes that you are wearing. You would think the freshness of water pouring or even dripping would cleanse the mind. But when it hits the parched weeds and grass, the smell of the aroma could have changed. The muddy creeks and the pools after the "rain of ashes" brought out an odor that is distinguished from the dryness that once was there.

This visionary view of the "sparkling glitter" landing on your head during a hot sunny afternoon puts a "youthful glow on your smile." A cool purity of this "fresh rain influenced me into dancing" with the sparkles that were falling from the sky. The feeling of coolness on your aching skin brings "laughter to you and to the clouds above."

This overwhelming discovery "by chance" allows me to meet the propulsions of these small particles that were dancing on my face. While embracing this view, you happen to see the colors that have changed as you look toward the sky. Will these tiny little droplets permit you to perceive your own identity?

A stranger following the course of the day was looking at the display. His observance asked, "Where is the providence of my stance?" Will the unknown receive an answer that satisfies the curious nature of their character? Being motionless in an idling stance while pondering at the "clouds in the sky" seems to make one wonder if we'll see rain.

Does the enjoyment of its wetness sprinkle excitement for those of you who want to come out and play? This enlighten force of splash has you looking at the dashing grounds "while watching" it has a tendency to just wash away.

A fortune was noticed as the "brightness was showing the shininess" of its silver lining. As the sky was forming a smile, you could see the glaze covering its eye's. Have we looked upon a dream that once was written that was only found in plays?

While I stood there "under the clouds of rain," there was a harmony singing a song for those who can hear.

The light within the darkness sent lyrics of enchantment, whistling tunes of delightful melodies. The strings of these instruments were tickling your ears as the horns echoed out messages that sent you walking on air. This idling moment makes me wonder as it caresses the uprightness of our delay, allowing a wet falling substance to hit my face!

Should we be inspired by the warmth of "rain on a hot sunny day?" Does the enjoyment sprinkle its mystery showing "smiles with a glaze?" Or can we find favor with the wetness that may form tears? Has the complexity been introduced to make things harder for us to understand?

This creative process that allows water to fall from the sky can be amazing, just thinking about it!

But somehow it has replaced our joy into a dark dreariness that we happen to see! As it approaches from a distance, you notice the grayness of your surroundings becoming darker. Focusing your eyes on the blurriness as the "gust of winds were howling, blowing," and tossing you around like wet rags in a tub! This had you pondering how strong the "rain and stormy winds" have become. These "clouds of darkness" have stepped in causing you to go blind, resembling a gloomy appearance that no one could hold!

Will the "loudness of thunder" wake up his shiny partner that likes to send "bolts of spark across the sky?" A strong withering abrasion was rubbing against the clothes you're wearing as you saw the "force of the storm" sneezing mucous from the abruption of its cold, "exhaling its breath," sending wet liquid out to those who are below!

Now you can see his mouth as he begins to open his nostrils so he can "inhale for another breath." Will he send another round of darkness with the "winds shaking and quivering its invisible coil?" A sudden twist of its glory could be announced through the sounds of its choice. Who can close the mouth that "blows out his laughter?" Do we dare talk with the "winds of time," asking can you ease off a little?

The "clouds that roam with the sky" has filled up their sponge, waiting for permission to empty the condensed liquid that has filled up their foggy chambers. This excessive fluid has caused it to become overcrowded as it starts to show agony, causing a deep-bluish color forming on his face. Can he be persuaded to let it just rain with a gentle flow crossing the plains? Or will he preserve us for another day as he flies by looking for another place? Or could this rapid falling substance engulf us with its violent rage?

Hopefully he can keep his anger under control and not flood the grounds that we're standing on. We see from his discomfort that he's ready to pour out his cup that could lead to a long miserable day. Has he absorbed all the passages in his porous skin? Can he find relief in his gaseous form! Is there something he could take to relieve his congestion?

"Oh my," now we're talking to the clouds as if they were our brother or sister. I wonder is there something that could cause him to burp. This illusion of "blown up clouds" that are bursting at the seams has brought some weird thoughts to your brain.

When the clouds have emptied the watery contents it held, it begins by showing a brilliant assortment of colors flowing across the sky. The "crescent quarter-moon ring" with its dazzling shades of color shows off its spectrum in layers of lines. "Will the rainbow shine" its glowing image to hold back the "clouds of rain!"

In the Green Book

Is THIS JUST a feeling that came up to me and "said hello?" And if it is, why is it going down the inner side of a wall, leaving me behind as I stare at the door? Can you feel what I feel? And do you see what we see? Have we heard something like this before? Sometimes there are things that come along, asking, "Are you him that we saw the other day while we were riding on the wings of an eagle?"

We would look at them strangely, saying, "Are you talking to me? Or have you been staring out the window to long?"

As the gusty wind went by, it turned to us and started whistling in the sky. It would come around to blast a sound and create a suggestion that's been hinting to you all along. This whirling motion was spinning as if it was performing a dance while coming up to echo a tune for you.

Watching it swirl and twirl as it snags a victim that doesn't seem to understand the aftereffects, it keeps looking for a way out so it could breathe again. Have we been entrapped in a plastic cage overwhelmed by the lack of freedom that's been known to us? Watch the sojourner who comes and goes as he pleases, and then he finds himself riding a skateboard before he slips away.

Who has gathered some know-how of when to flee as they see a twist that's been shaken…the bark off the trees?

If you want it, let it free and walk away. Don't lose your mind that's been inside your head, wondering how we could get away. Has one ever held the fascination of beauty in their hands? Can your emotions open and move by a charm that we find irresistible?

Could the sunshine of a beaming light open your hearts to a narrow passage "we have not yet found?" Or have we been stuck in a block of ice freezing our asses off? Are we supposed to be infallible? "Who's kidding who?" Have the daydreams put you in a fantasy land, thinking of candy canes?

These delusional onsets like standing on a pillar of gold could this billow upset and spill the applecart that we've been pushing all along?

A chuckle from humor may ask, "Where do the funnies run to?"

I've been sitting in a puddle of mud waiting for it to dry up so we could get a good impression of what some of our neighbors may look like.

Looking in a mirror and answering the outer door, asking, "Where did you come from? Have we met someplace before?"

Have the broken pieces of yesterday show up to give you another chance?

Is there a way to overcome a feeling of being a lost and lonely child with no confidence left?

"Have we read the comics yet?"

Have we been stranded inside a bucket in a hole and found ourselves covered up in snow, and we could not find a way out? While working yourself up, you managed to bring your head above ground. As you find yourselves buried in snow from your neck on down, a slushy bulldog comes up slobbering on you. You holler, "Get help before you drown me!" But he keeps licking your face.

The dog finally answers you and says, "Which way should I go, George?"

We told him, "Anywhere, as long as you bring somebody back that doesn't slobber on me."

The bulldog said, "Okay," and turned around and ran away. Before we could say howdy-dowdy-dandy three times, he was back with a cat.

We looked at each other for a few minutes, and I finally asked, "Now how are you guys going to help me?"

The cat came over and licked my face and said, "Meow."

The bulldog asked, "Did I do good, George?" She doesn't slobber.

Do you feel the frost while you're standing on thin ice, wondering to yourselves how in the world did we get into this mess? You may think, "Oh my goodness, how we have tried so hard, and we still find ourselves getting confused on what we should do." Does this sound familiar when you have a loss of words, and you still ponder what could have went wrong.

You find yourself shaking your head from side to side with a disappointing look on your face. Having a half-hearted grin, you realize some are doing the best they can. You ask, "How this can be?" We thought the plan was simple enough for anybody to follow. "Oh dear," I guess we'll need to work on our messages to make them idiot proof.

But you still have this oh-my look that you can't seem to get rid of.

You question the outcome, thinking, "I hope it doesn't end with little pieces of my head scattered all over the room, as if it was a jigsaw puzzle waiting to be found."

What if you can see yourself in the green book of fantasies when you decide to open it up?

We seem to hear things from this book, saying, "It's time to open me up." It's shouting, "I can only scream for so long. What are you doing out there?"

There is a magical dream of a thousand wishes that could come your way. But you don't see them until the green book has been opened, and only one wish will come to you each day. Sadly enough you can't pick your dream; the wish of the dream picks you.

Will you take a chance for an unexpected occurrence to be with you for a day? Has your curiosity provoked you to a point of excitement, urging you to open the book of charms? While reaching for this book, you notice your fingers are getting sweaty just thinking about opening to a page. This book has a glossy greenish-silver cover accented with golden fringes hanging off its borders and tassels to mark a space.

As you slowly open the green book, an unforeseen image springs forth, a bright light that has you hiding your eyes. An image of a ghostly smoke floats above, and the book quickly closes, and the mist flashes away. While rubbing your eyes from the dampness coming off the mist, there stands a pale stranger in front of us. Clothed in black attire from his top hat down to his shoes, and he was hiding his face behind his cape.

Laughing with a haughty sound, he drops his cape from his face, and you see someone with contemptuous cold eyes with "reddish-blue rings" around the sockets and lips. Frothy foam was spewing from his mouth and teeth as his ghastly appearance seemed to change with "reddish-green smoke" blowing out his nostrils.

After seeing a fantasy book of dreams come to life, you may say to yourselves, "Have we been in a scary nightmare lately? Who is this creature with bad breath?" What would the dark depths want with me? Is this the page we picked out from the green book?"

Well, that's what we get for eating those hot taco's last night! And just think, we will have to spend the whole day with this wannabe demonic appearance in front of me. We asked him, "What do you want with us?"

He looked at me with his red streak eyes and said, "Don't you recognize me? I'm playing a part in a play."

"What play is that?" was my reply back to him.

He stared at me astounded and implied don't you know, "You opened the book and brought me here!"

I told him, "We have no idea. There wasn't time for me to look at the page, let alone the story."

With a confused look on his face, he replied, "The only life I have is in that play, and you pulled me out of that part. How do I get back to where we belong? You and everything around are new to me."

As he sat down with his elbows on his knees and his hands under his chin, it appeared he was worried that he would never see the play he was in. He looked as though he lost his best friend.

With concern I insisted, "Don't be so sad. It's not as bad as what you think. You'll be back in the play the next day."

I tried to cheer him up, saying, "We were amazed by your performance when we first met."

He looked up, startled, glanced at me, and blurred out, "Yea, right." Then he stated, "But we didn't frighten you as were supposed to like we scared those in the play!"

"Well," I answered back, "you caught me by surprise and shocked me to a point that we couldn't move or shout with fear. He said, "Go on, you're just saying that to be nice."

"Oh no, no, you did have an effect on my emotions. I thought we were watching a terrifying movie!"

He answered back, "Really?"

"You know it!"

After these exchanges of words, he seemed to be a little more relaxed. At this time, I thought we will tell him. While staring at him, I told him, "You will be in the book tomorrow, so don't worry. You'll be back in the play."

He jumped up excited and said, "Are you for sure?"

"Yes, I believe so. They say my dream is good for only one day."

Then the mystery of the wish goes back to the page we picked inside the green book. He shouted, "Excellent! I hope we didn't miss any rehearsals. I couldn't help myself from laughing, and we laughed so hard watching this Dr. Jekyll image dancing around in circles with so much enthusiasm, looking as if he came back to life.

While we were enjoying the good news, I pondered about this character that belongs in a play, and after a few more hours, I'll probably never see him again. So I asked him, "What is the part that you play in the story?"

He stopped to think while he took his top hat off and started rubbing his forehead. He was stunned, and said he couldn't remember.

"Well, then what is your name?"

Lightly scratching his temple, he kind of grinned and said, "I don't remember that either."

Collecting my thoughts together, I decided to ask, "How do you know that you're in a play?"

"Since you brought that up, what I remember was, we were acting as a fiend trying to frighten somebody that was a cast in the play. But I don't recall who!" I told him if we knew what the title of the story was, we would read it later to see how good you were. He got somewhat choked up and said, "You would do that for me?"

"Sure, I would, since we met you coming from a mystic book of dreams."

He told me, "I'll try very hard to remember." But in the meantime, he was practicing his role-acting on some scenes from a sketch. Befuddled with curiosity had me staring in the sky, watching this stranger play, acting as if there was nothing else on his mind. I couldn't help myself but kept wondering why!

While glancing at him, I was being amazed by the ability of his skills. He was showing strong verbal quality from that temperamental scornful voice he has.

Then the hour came without any warning or notice. The green book opened, and a mist of fog came out to take this actor back. As I glared at this supernatural phenomenon, it quickly enveloped him, and as it was going back in the green book, I heard him saying "sni...d-d-d," and the book had closed.

It was as if he had "one foot in and one foot out" of the green book. But what was he trying to tell me, saying snid?" Was it his name or part of a title? Well, I guess we'll find out someday."

I think I'll wait another day before we pick another wish from the mystery book.

The Clouds, the Rain, and I

It was a hot sticky day of traveling in the desert as I was wearing my shorts with sew-on flannel patches that kept the jeans together and a tank top where I was burning my shoulders to a crisp; that's when I happened to find myself lost in a desert. In this shiny dust bowl after entering a somewhat barren land, I was walking to a place that I didn't have any idea where, and now I'm suspicious of where I came.

My sense of direction has led me a stray trying to find my correction! My selection has caused me to lose my perception!

Puzzled by this, now I know I was looking for my perfection!

My question was, "Will somebody help me with a suggestion?"

Talking to myself, "Are we going to go back around to find you, to help me out with my inception?"

Standing there confusing myself after walking for a while in the heated sand, I was glancing around with my hand tilted sideways on my forehead blocking out the sun.

We were looking for any signs of life that we could go to. Those mystical waves coming up out of the sand were floating in the air, making it hard to see straight. The sun's powerful heat continually beating upon my skin; it felt as if we were cooking ourselves on a barbeque pit. The perspiration that was dripping off me, we could fill a cup up in no time.

Staggering in my footprints, the sand seemed to sink below my ankle line on each step I took. One thing I realized was that we ran out of water three hours back. Only if I had saved some water for later, I wouldn't be drenched and seeing wavy steam lines.

It was time to take a break. I was getting tired and exhausted from walking in the sand. While sitting on the hot sand, I made sure

I wasn't exposing any skin to the sand; it probably would of burn the skin off my hide. Wiping the sweat off my face using my T-shirt, I happen to glance at a hill side dune; there seemed to be a shadowy reflection over the hill.

Thinking I may see mirages, I took another quick glimpse over the hill and saw a tall object glaring off the sun from a distance. I thought I'll walk toward that place.

The heat was starting to get unbearable while dragging my feet up this hill. Steamy waves rising toward the skyline kind of put me in a dreamy sensation.

In this warm stuffy terrain, the air seemed to become denser and a little harder to breathe.

My destination seemed to look farther away than what we thought. In my delirious mind, I was getting "closer and closer" with each step I took. When we approached within eyesight, I saw it, one of the biggest oak trees I ever seen.

"Glaring at its gleaming leaves and branches" made me think I'm going to sit down under the shade of this big oak tree and rest. With an awe expression, "I saw grass that encircled this nice moist tree." While resting, we laid our head against the trunk and closed our eyes trying to relax from this hot day.

About the time we started to sleep, a strange behavior within the vicinity had woke me up. Looking all around, we pondered, "Where are these sounds coming from?"

There was nothing in sight, not even the wind was blowing. There was no living creature crawling or running across the horizon of this open domain. I kept glancing for movement or noises, but it was quiet. I thought to myself we must be hearing things.

As we lay back once again, "I heard snickering giggles and short burst of laughter" surrounding me from the air! There also was "muttering voices" you could barely perceive. This made me think out loud and wonder, "What's happening?" It was as if someone was pulling practical jokes on my account.

With a hasty glance, I looked upon the sky, amazed only to see "two lonely clouds," and they seemed to be bumping into each other while they were smiling. So I sat there staring at them for a while; there wasn't anything else to see or do.

Whatever the noise was somehow it disappeared, but this put a suspicious thought in my head. Well, I decided to lie back with my head against the tree and tried to rest again.

After a few minutes passed by, I heard a "squeak commenced to tapping," and the "loudness of footsteps started rapping, the thunder sounding off with a clippity-clap-clop" commotion was opening up with a curious melody being drawn out!

While glaring up, I was hearing a tone of harmony as if it was playing in a choir band. The song seemed to remain the same when the action in the sky started performing some unusual ritual that I have never seen before!

At this time, I noticed a "small side hutch window open" between the two clouds, a hand throws something, and as it flies out, then the hutch proceeded to close again!

This window had done this several times every few minutes making me hesitate and watch to see what was going to happen next. I got a glimmer of what was being thrown out; it looked like a sheet of paper, and it would float tossing and rocking like a child's cradle in the sky. The way those two clouds were carrying on it looked as if there was some sort of a message being addressed to them.

When the "window had closed" completely, it seem to blend in with the sky. There was no trace of it ever being there! I was astonished. Where did the window go?

Staring at the sky, the event seemed to come to an end. "I saw the two clouds" started talking to each other about the note that was thrown out of the window. I interrupted them to ask, "What type of clouds are you?"

They answered back with a tone of anger in their voice saying, "Cumulus!" Then they commenced on talking again. With curiosity on my mind, I pondered with a question, "What are your names?" The one cloud roared back and said, "What is this twenty question? Now leave us alone. We have serious business to discuss, and then it will be our playtime."

So I sat beside the tree to relax, and we couldn't quite hear what the discussion was all about. But I was inquisitive about what was on the paper that "flew out of the window."

The one cloud said, "Well, it's time to have fun." And he began shooting cloud balls at the other cloud. So the cloud being shot at started throwing smoke bubbles back at his murky pal.

Every so often, they would glance down to see if there was anybody listening to their conversation while echoing their voices with laughter. They were commenting how warm it's getting, being so close to the sun and wondering, "When will our master be ready for us to let it rain?"

One was mentioning, "Even my suspended ice crystals are breathing heavy. Soon they will need to be cooled down and freshen up! If he doesn't let us cool off here, I wish he would send us along our way where we can."

The other cloud responded, "You got that right. I'm burning up to a boiling point!"

One of them mentioned, "We are floating into a sea of sweat. I'm turning to steam while we sit in this spot!"

As they searched below, one of them said, "Even those down there have more sense than us to stick around here."

About this time, the small window opened and shot out an object, and the clouds saw and read it. Then the window closed!

Suddenly the roar of thunder started to roll across the sky, and the sparks of lightning were flashing across the plains, and now the clouds had permission to begin the rain!

Run in Where

The road is in style. Can you carry it for a while? Or is the load too heavy, and you find yourselves lost in traffic? But you can't seem to resist the view it shows looking toward the swing in path.

The glamour of a twisted unknown seems to persuade you with unruly romance. Will you see some sunshine as you ride down to unlock a lonely door? This feeling of emptiness chooses to follow, even into the uncharted waters that have no desire. You keep saying, "We need to get away. Let's fly away to the next road we see. Will there be a tomorrow that can get you to the place you want to be? Or do you find yourselves losing time inside your head, and you ask, "Am I stuck in this shell?"

Being alone trying to escape the things of the past, it's saying, "Hurry---hurry---! Now don't let it catch up to you." It could squeeze the living daylights out of your hidden secrets. These secrets that keep haunting you, will it ever pass or does it keep pushing you into a corner of glass?

Riding in a fast lane at a high speed may wake you up wondering, "Where am I running too?" Is there an in-between space we could keep a steady course with? Or do we feel like a stranger walking on a crooked line, and it keeps moving without warning? Do I need to ask myself, "have you been hearing things that seems to lurk inside your head? And you find yourselves drifting, not knowing which way to go?" A blind feeling has come over you, wondering, "What am I doing here? And how did this happen?"

I'm looking for my clothes and shoes, so I may get ready to run "to the next door." I feel like a boy wearing high-heeled shoes. Or are they pumps for we don't know? They sure slow me down. Wearing the same shoes day in and day out with no place to go, how do I get out of the cold?

This place you find yourselves in could be worse than the place you started with. Have your senses been taken away? Or are you content with the condition you woke up in? Will they take me for a ride, strip me of everything I have, even my pride?

Will a sparkle ever show up so I could tell one from the other?

If we had everything, would that make me king? Would that fulfill my dream and let me rule my life for another day? As you open a door, you found a chance to walk through and run along another path. The road you choose seems to get you lost.

Feeling like a beggar crying, asking, "Please don't turn out the lights. I'm trying to get out of the dark!"

The shutters of our eyes seem to be distracted with curiosity, wondering if they are open or close. And where do we stand? Confusion has set in, and we noticed our actions seem to be pondering. You may ask yourself, "Are we coming or going? I hope we're not flying in circles. "Oh my, we forgot to choose. Have we been fooling ourselves again? But it does seem to help when you have nothing else to lose. These blankets in life have been kept tight, and now I can't see anymore.

These illusions of self-doubt have come to visit me, and now they have overstayed their welcome. Watching the reasons that seek your attention seems to get in the way. "Why would this trembling anxiety keep following me around?" Now it says he has a friend that he would like to introduce me to? I hear the piano playing a tune of regret; they both seem to have a field day on my expense.

Is this really living? Sometimes it's hard to tell. Well, it's time to look for the next road. Now where is that confounded door? Has life's uncertainty come as a sorrow? And you decide to wait for tomorrow, but it's no better than the day in front of you?

Somehow we seem to make love until we weep, not knowing will there be a satisfaction or will there be tears? Have you found the woman in you has changed? Something's never stay the same. Sometimes I wonder if the woman in you is worried about the woman in me!

This delusion from the shadow stays within trying to hide the truth! The shame would follow. Have you lost your mind in a puzzle? If I could get all I want, would that be enough? Or do you still think you got less? Sometimes I feel lost, and I'm waiting for my breath to show up so I can run again. Other times I can't move my feet; it feels like I'm stuck in the ground somehow like a tree.

I thought I knew it all, but somehow my ideas and my courage have disappeared. It's been walking the streets looking for the next road to meet.

Walking on top of a fence lets me see which way we'll fall. Will we keep running in a direction to a place we don't know? Has life drained the slightest ambitions you might have had? And you find out the things you wanted to do may not be so easy, and it usually comes with a price? Are you still looking for a door that you can slip through hoping you may find the right road?

Maybe you scolded yourselves saying, "It's time to put the brakes on. I'm tired of running zero to sixty in three seconds." Now you find yourselves going zero to sixty trying to make up for lost time!

"Oh my," the consequences you put yourself through so you may ease the mind. How they have pulled me like a string running up and down with yo-yos! Why do certain things turn out the way they did? Somehow you lost track of what you could have done next. Seeing yourselves constantly spinning looking at different directions, contemplating, "Which way should I run to now?" Does this feel like living or have we been dreaming?

When you see the bottom of your cup, you may realize time is getting short. Are people like a mosquito that tries to get to know you but become a nuisance? For every time they land on your skin, they want to kiss you with a sting, saying, "Are you my friend?" Will we ever slow down enough to watch it shine instead of running here to there to see how fast we can go?

An Unseen

THE ENTANGLEMENT THAT persists while it was flowing began to rear its ugly head. Who gave it permission to try to ensnare you? This unforeseen event came along to signal its intentions. Stillness was moving to yield itself to a path that one has not noticed or one could not fight against. Who brought this before our sight? Has this been the norm watching an invisible wall standing erect not allowing anything to pass or go? Would the images or even the emotions of someone's viewpoint affect their decision of what may come? Has our vision showed us partiality that may bring us a doubtful outcome?

During a brief intercession, the attributes discovered led you to look at the next event.

After glancing at a blur, we happen to see things that others didn't, and I wondered to myself, "Do I actually see this or am I imagining an unknown that's not there?"

Of course, this has you asking, "Can we keep this going this way?" Certain foresights allow me to engage on what to do next.

There are conditions I found when we were driving down the road; it felt as though "my eyes can't see," but my mind wants to cry out loud! This unfounded rarity seems to keep my brain focused, asking, "How did this all come into play!"

As we were walking on the streets to a store one day, I noticed nobody around. We didn't see anything, but I heard "voices shouting about." The noises of people shuffling around inside the premise led me to believe the store was open. When I approached the door, there was a sign hanging, saying, "We're closed,." And when we looked around, there was nothing in sight. The day turned into the middle of night. I asked myself, "Where did the whole day disappear to?"

After waking up this morning, I turned the radio on, and they said it will be a bright sunny day. Eventually we started looking out the window, and it was a cloudy cold day. I gazed at the idea, "Where did they get their report? The sun refused to shine. Well, I thought what's wrong with this picture."

If they were to tell me the mountain lived in the sea, I would say, "Let it be because I don't mind."

Should a tornado come by and pick me up? I would ride the breeze to set me free and tell them it was about time!

I could look upon this as if we got caught in a whirlwind where I can't catch my breath, and "I would say the wind wants to play also!"

Putting up with this "allusive three-dimensional vision of the unseen" has me pondering and talking to myself. In my cold sweat, I've been longing to dismiss the suspense, for day by day and night after night feels like I'm losing time, finding myself walking on a tightrope, and I can't seem to get off.

It's been a long time since I've seen my shadow following me around, certain places it disturbs me, thinking I'm walking naked without a care in the world.

I had a vision one night as I've seen an illusion; thousands upon thousands of candles lit up on the sands, and they were slipping one by one into the sea, and I thought, "Is that what it takes to light up the seas?"

Observing this dilemma has me thinking, "Have I lost a screw or am I a (six-o-one) mental case? Either way, I've been losing my mind!

I feel like a bird with a busted wing, and we have no time to spare. The walls are coming in seeing if they can squeeze any patience I have away.

Gathering my thoughts and storing them in the shade, hoping they don't get too much sun, will be a helping hand, if they don't get fried up.

This deep penetration that exists with a keenness of the mind shows insight that belongs in the sky, roaming along the ocean tops looking for the tidal waves.

When my vision came back to behold, I found myself along an old colonial wooden ship with shipmates in old scraggily clothes, a flag that flew in black with skull and crossbones waving in the breeze.

As I was on the top deck, we were watching to see what was going to happen next.

The captain with his black beard and patched eye started shouting, even barking out orders to get the ship lined up for its course. Now the captain and helmsman stirred the rudder to help set the ships channel. While the sailors were running along the deck, they were resetting the sails and lines to tie things off so they may set the rugged caravel ships way.

One of them shouted to the other mates, "Home sweet home. We're on our way."

Another swab said, "Where are you going, Molly dear?"

The other hollered, "What's it to you, Moby Dick."

And they both started laughing. We've got the booty now, and the captain said, "We'll be diva it up soon."

When this vision started to diminish, my perception told me I was in a dream. I thought for a minute and said, "Oh, well, I don't mind."

After a period went by, I found my vision was looking and pondering at a ceremony of the decease. They called him "Willie the Blimp." They laid him to rest in a special way, sent him off in his finest style.

He was riding in his casket mobile that he drove a while. As he was in "his Cadillac coffin," sitting in the driver's style seat, he had diamonds on his fingers, hundred-dollar bills flashing from his vest. And his Cadillac had flowers on the wheels with flashing headlights as it ran its course to the tomb of his gravesite.

Now this was bizarre in a special strange way; he's going to be buried after riding in town in his Cadillac coffin with all the luxurious trimmings, along with his bent imagination.

As I relinquished my mind from these visions unseen, and with my normal eyesight reappearing again, I received instructions to visit "cloud-nine" sitting on the end of a rainbow!

I admonished within a sparely demise, saying, "How am I going to get there? My vision has given me rest."

He mentioned to me, "When you have received your rest, you'll be in the air flying along the landscape to find your new destiny!"

When I woke up, we noticed our vision has gotten stronger after the rest we had, and the next thing I realized, we were on our way through the air to "cloud-nine."

The speed we were traveling was alarming. At this rate, it put us there ahead of schedule, and when we eventually got there to see this marvel, we had time to admire the gleaming brightness it was showing.

These splendors of glowing colors had me wondering, "How many different shades are there?"

As we were counting the layers of different colors that were upon each other, we came up with the "number seven." I told myself when we got here, we would make a point to count the clouds from the peak on down.

When we came to the end of the rainbow, we only counted six! So I asked where the rest of the clouds were. "I'm on cloud-six!"

I was told from a voice inside my head, "Do not worry!"

"Well, I voiced my opinion and said, "If six turned out to be nine, I don't care. Let it be, for I don't mind."

So what am I to do now? We visited cloud-six, and I saw the exquisite colors of light from the rainbow with its sparkling glowness and flattery glaze.

I heard a voice saying, "Come up hither. I want to talk to you." When we reached the gates that were floating in the clouds of the highest mountain peaks, we had permission to enter.

His thunderous voice implied, you have had a great privilege of witnessing these sights. Do you not appreciate the visions that you have been shown? For you have been impeccable on your choices, there are many more in stored if you choose to do so.

You have been in this top visionary field for quite a while, being picked as an expert in the "unseen visionary exploratory research program should be an honor.

I replied back with an admirable thank you, "And as much as this is commendable, we need an opportunity for a change." He answered back with authority and wanted to know what the problem was!

As much as we have enjoyed the traveling and sightseeing, my mind would like to lead a normal life, and I want to give it a chance.

He said, "If that is your wish, you may give it a try, but don't be surprised if your casual redundancy becomes boring, and the repetitious outcome becomes a sight for sore eyes."

He followed up and said, "If you were to change your mind, just let me know, and I'll hear you, and we can talk about this again."

I said, "Thank you, your majesty, we will keep that in mind."

Blissful Fortune of Rain

IN THE BOOK of memories, one may recall the joy of exquisite loveliness in the delicacy form of a flower with unique colors after a sprinkle of rain running across the blooming of its radiance.

It opens and wakes the nature for maturity to begin and flourish a blossom to gleam its splendor.

One notices the bee traveling from one flower to another pollinating the gift to thrive amongst the plants.

The beauty and the sweet scent of its smell brings freshness that excides a wonderful pleasure and a youthful glow.

Somehow it has a tendency upon sight to quiet one's soul and peace lies within.

In weathers of severity may show an obstruction of life that may be unforgiving.

The quantities could pour down so hard as to damage this sensitive graceful softness.

This entity of rain believed by some could bring good or bad luck. I suppose like all, there chance of fate can be determined by its choice.

Success could be measured in the happiness it unfolds in the satisfaction of its gratitude.

This is a personal prosperity of your desire that one may observe. A contentment of joyous delight may spark charming excitement that draws a pretty picture.

Some may look at rain as being a sorrow and ask, "What will we do today that can be objective?"

The plants may be dancing, enjoying the pleasantness, singing along the freshness that cools them down from the excessive heat.

The dryness from the sun can be painful amongst the nature of its growth. We should be fortunate to admire the rain that sustains the living to maintain a favor which will be thankful.

A Shadow Moved

Standing and leaning against an office building on the corner of where my honey works, it was lunch hour, and I saw a man pass by me, and I didn't think much about it. For it happens to get a little crowded at this time of day. People were walking up and down the street going here to there. But this particular individual seemed to have gotten my attention, for the sun was out, and it was about eleven thirty in the morning. We were in the middle of the square, just on the other side of the street from where the governor's mansion is located.

While I was waiting to take her to lunch, he passed by me, and I noticed there were two shadow images following him! The rest of the people that passed by, they only had one. As I was glancing at one of the two shadows and observing it very closely, the one shadow turned and waved his hand at me, recognizing I was following them.

I stopped and shook my head in disbelief, and the shadow proceeded to go along with the shadow he was with! Profound by the man that the two shadows were following, I glanced at his attire, and he was wearing a gray suit, shoes, and hat, didn't see his face as he turned around in the opposite direction. Silently he approached the street in front of me, and there was a bench you could sit on while waiting; that is where he decided to sit.

When I came a little closer, I saw the two shadows sitting beside him on the same side. He was looking at his watch and viewing the street. I guess he was waiting on somebody like I was a few moments ago.

At this time, the shadow knew I was staring at him. He turned and nodded his head back and forth, then he commenced to taking the original position. While he was sitting there, he took out part of a newspaper that he had in his jacket pocket, so when he opened it up to read, I still couldn't see his face, but the two shadows demonstrated they had a newspaper too. But I didn't know who was actually reading it and the one who was just going through the motion. When the man got through one page and turned the page, the shadows followed suit, so it made it harder for me to pick him out, and I think he knew it.

As I started pacing from side to side wondering, "How am I going to get this shadow moving again?" Then out of the corner of my eye, I saw him standing on the bench seat with his arms folded and the newspaper closed while the man and the other shadow were still sitting down with their paper open.

I began to think, "Oh my, he's got guts. Doesn't anybody else see him? Apparently not!"

That was about the time Sally yelled at me and said, "What are you doing down there?"

I waved to her to come over here. She shrugged her head and came down and asked, "What are you doing, Henry? Where are we going to eat lunch at?"

I looked back at the bench where the shadow was, and he must have sat back down and had the paper open again! Then I told Sally about the story. She looked at me like I had flipped out or was beyond myself. I pointed the shadow out, and Sally, with excitement, said, "Where? I don't see anything."

And I casually said, "Right there!"

And now she thought I was joking with her because she didn't see anything peculiar, except the way I was acting!

I tried my best to assure her this was real. I ended up pleading with her, then she finally said, "Okay, whatever, but I'm still hungry, and I only have an hour for lunch, so are you coming with me?"

"Wait a minute, Sally, I'm going over there to find out what is actually happening. I'll be right back."

"Well, hurry then, Henry, I'm not going to waste my lunch hour on this!"

So I went over to approach this man and his shadows that were sitting on the bus bench, and this was when he got up and started walking down the street, and the shadows followed. Now one shadow turned around and put his hands on his head while looking at me!

This responsive act brought attention to me and made me think this was a dauntless move on his part! He's deliberately insinuating that he can get away without any repercussions. Then the shadow turned back around and went in his typical format following the other shadow. The man went down the street, standing in front of a restaurant when a woman showed up. They seemed to be greeting one another before entering through the door. That was when one shadow disappeared, and the other shadow looked as though it flew up into the air and left the scene.

I stared amazed at what I just saw, well, somewhat stunned. We thought, "I guess it's gone!" So I began to walk back where I had left Sally, and I apologized to her about my inconsideration. She glanced at me in a somewhat spiteful way. Then she reminded me, "It's getting late, and we need to hurry. Let's go to the pizza palace. It's about a block down the street."

I smiled at her and replied, "That works for me."

And when I turned to walk toward that direction, she noticed something behind me. When I began walking, the shadow tipped his hand from his head like he was introducing himself to Sally. During this short interaction, the shadow then proceeded to follow the other shadow acting as though nothing special happened.

Now at this point, Sally immediately stopped in her tracks, wondering, "Is this for real?" Then she saw I had two shadows following me! Her voice piped up shockingly and said, "Henry, do you realize that you have two shadows following you!"

I looked back at Sally and saw her face; it turned as pale as a ghost wearing a white sheet. While she was staring behind me was when I decided to turn my head around, and I only saw one shadow. Mine! I told her, "Sweetie, I only see my shadow." She looked dismayed as if her whole concept of reality just flew out the window. I kept playing ring-around-the-rosy turning around in slow circles, hoping to see this shadow that's been following me.

Then I stood there thinking, "Why can Sally see him, and I can't?" This made me wonder if that's what happened with the last man in the gray suit; he simply didn't see the other shadow. I was profound what next! A tingling sensation blurred out. "What if he could hear me!" I asked, "Sally, is he still behind me?"

"Yes, he's lying on the ground with the other shadow. Of course, I couldn't tell you one from the other."

Perplexed about asking this, I thought, "Sally, what if this shadow can hear us?" I told her, "He can't talk to us but how about hearing us?"

The baffled expression on her face with her eyes squinting like I said something amusing was priceless. She inquired how that could be possible!

"Let's just say it is, then what?" Sally just stood there listening to what I was saying, thinking to herself, "Do you honestly believes the shadow can hear and understand what you're saying?"

I told her, "I don't know, but I'm willing to give it a try, besides I'm curious of what he is doing here and why!"

Sally with her sensibility thought, "How you are going to manage any form of communication with a shadow?"

And of course, I with my vivid imagination thought I would play some form of Sam Spade a private-eye detective in which made Sally laugh with hysteria. She giggled and thought, "Okay, Dick Tracy, what's the game plan?"

I asked, "Sally, quit laughing. This is serious business."

She said, "I can't help myself seeing Sam Spade in the flesh." But evidently when she glanced back down on the ground, she noticed the one shadow with his hands behind his head in a relaxed position while they were lying on the ground. At that time, she looked at me with an uncanny expression saying, "He seems to hear what we're saying!"

She nervously asked me, "What are we going to do?"

I put my index finger to my lips and motioned to Sally. "Come here, and I'll whisper it in your ear. Let me think about this for a minute or two."

While we were both studying on the situation, Sally came up with an idea. She whispered to me, "Why couldn't we use hand signals to try to communicate with the shadow?"

Then Sally perked up and said, "Why do we need to whisper?" Sally caught me off guard, and I pondered from Sally's remark. Looking rather confused, I muttered, "I'm not for sure anymore."

"Well, I'm thinking if you want to talk with the shadow, he needs to know himself, doesn't he?"

I was starting to realize Sally was making more sense than I was! Excited about the idea of talking with a shadow, I thought and inquired to Sally, "How are we going to understand what he's trying to say and what he's trying to tell us?"

She said with a smile, "You will need to be a little more diplomatic," as she was smirking about the very idea of me being diplomatic. In fact, Sally was starting to laugh about the very idea of me playing a congressman. She thought, "Oh yeah, Mr. inspirational diplomacy with a feather stuck in his hat. I can see it now, Mr. President. Welcome home in bringing peace and tranquility." And she must have laughed for what seem like an eternity.

I with a grin on my face told Sally, "I think you are having way too much fun about this whole thing while I'm trying to bring some seriousness to this circumstance." That made Sally's laugh even louder!

The whole episode had the shadow lying there with his hands on his hips as if he was waiting for the next motion from me. "Let's go back to the suggestion of hand signals, in which I thought was a pretty good idea," I replied.

Sally quit her giggling and implied, "Well, you will need to ask questions and get some form of answer. How do we propose to do this?"

I gingerly quoted to Sally, "We'll need to think about this because I don't know!"

Sally seemed to understand the burden I must be in and took my hand and held it firmly. She comforted my indecisiveness and murmured, "We'll figure something out."

I asked Sally, "How do we get the shadow to respond to a question that we can all understand, and we know he uses hand signals? So, so how about we say a yes question that you put your hands on your head and the no answers you fold your arms together! Because it seems like every time I see him do something, he's moving his hands, arms, or head."

Evidently Sally noticed me talking to myself. I said, "When I glanced at him, he was standing on the bench with his arms folded, and he has nodded his head at me. So why not? What do you think, Sally?"

Sally gazed at me and told me, "I don't have a clue of what you're rambling about. You lost me. He anxiously blurred out that he can move on his own accord, and there is something weird about what he can do!"

I looked at Sally, then at the shadow, and suggested, "Let's test it out."

Something else crossed my mind, so I asked the shadow, "I'm going to give you a series of questions, and you will answer them yes or no!"

I told him, "If it is a yes answer, you put both hands on your head. Well, shadow, do you understand the yes-and-no answers?" And he used one hand and put it on his head; Sally saw it and got so excited and told me, "It seems to work." But I reminded her it was one hand not both, but her rebuttal was, "He listens better than some people that I know."

Then I told both of them, "If it is a no answer, then you fold your arms together, do we all understand?" The shadow went ahead and put his hand on his head.

Then Sally had the confidence of stating, "You can start with your first question now!"

I looked at her and thought, "Just calm down a little."

After a few minutes passed by, I finally said, "Okay, did you leave the last man in the gray suit because he was going into the restaurant?"

The shadow folded his arms together. Sally told me, "He said no."

I saw it and thought it would be yes for sure! Now that answer really baffled me. I was privately thinking to myself, "Is he playing with me, for he does seem to have a sense of humor?" So I asked him, "Did you want to follow me?"

He used one hand to put on his head, which meant yes. So I paused on that answer and wished I could ask him why!

Sally pondered, "Why you?"

With a concern look on my face, I said "that's what I'm searching for".

My third question I thought about for a few minutes, then I gazed at the shadow and said, "Were you forced to follow me because you lost the last shadow?"

He put one hand on his head. Now Sally heard and saw what happened with curiosity. She asked, "How did you know?"

And my reply was, "I didn't! But I remember what occurred at the restaurant. You see, Sally, the gray-suit man's shadow disappeared. Now he went up into the air and vanished out of sight. I guess looking for another shadow to follow, and I was the lucky guy because I saw it."

She said, "Now what are you going to do?"

I grimly looked back and answered, "Nothing because if I'm looking at this right, and I lose my shadow, then he'll have to leave to find another shadow to follow." And here I thought, I was somewhat frightened about him, but he must be going through a process he has to in order to survive if that's what you want to call it. But I think he is in some unknown channel caught within an unusual dilemma or is it inside another dimension? I don't know! Just thinking about it, he might have been someone else's shadow at one time, and somehow they got separated. Now he doesn't know where to go and who he belongs to."

"When you put it that way, Henry, I kind of feel sorry for him, like he's lost and can't find his way home."

I looked at Sally and said, "I'm sorry too."

And she said, "What for?"

"Well, we missed lunch, and you're late."

Section 2

Dreams from a Window

Waking Up on the Other Side

WHILE FOLLOWING IN the footsteps along a strange paved thorough-fare, I glanced down to see a cobblestone walkway that seemed to lead me to a circular fountain. With bushes and flowers arrayed in an exquisite and beautiful landscape, surrounding the borders was decorated with eloquent reddish-and-white-colored stone accenting an elaborate touch. The hummingbirds and bees were sharing the delicacy of what Mother Nature set before them, traveling from one flower to the next.

The colors of the scenery pictured must be what heaven looks like. I was absolutely flabbergasted in awe. I had to stand there for a few moments just to soak in the peaceful excitement I was enjoying.

On the side, there sat an old brown-colored slatted wooden bench with black iron circular arm rails on the ends. As I sat on the bench, I began to listen to the water from the fountain of youth, trickling alongside the bowls as it was dripping from one level to the next. When it reached the basin, it would swirl and swirl into circular motions with a quaint gurgle sound. The soft voice it was making felt as if you were being hypnotized. This soothing relaxation caused me to nod off and fall asleep.

I found myself sleeping on the bench in tranquility, resting with a cool breeze, and "dreaming of different exotic colors sparkling a shiny ray of sunshine on my face." A figment of my imagination must have gotten away; the glowing glory was spectacular of what I seen in my dream. Upon awakening, I looked at the "Graceland." I thought we were in! Somehow things have changed, and this was not what I saw the day before.

While collecting my thoughts, I noticed this wasn't a cobble-stone floor that encircled the fountain. It was a worn-out dirt path. And as I stared at the fountain, the nozzle head had enough algae and moss built on it to be almost closed off where it usually spews the water from.

The delicious bushes and flowers were so rotten away they reminded me of a hobo's pot of greens with turnips and secondhand radishes. The beautiful hewn stones that I saw earlier were discolored and cracked up in the overgrown slimy moss that covered them.

"Shuttering with surprise had me wondering with curiosity" as we looked around for any sign and asking ourselves, "What's this all about?" While we were trying to gather our senses, a thought came to mind, "Maybe I'm dreaming again?"

Looking within the scenery that surrounded me, I thought to myself, "We weren't drinking, and surely we aren't delusional. So what has happened? Because this is not the same."

I've decided this inner circle has changed. Let me go out to see if something seems different along the outer spaces. In my deranged superstitious mind, I started to gallivant along the outer edges of this unusual park, pondering and asking myself, "Is this where we came in last night?"

I was thinking (outside the box), "Could abnormalities of anxiety and a phobia have bases to put me in a neurosis disorder, for I don't seem to remember? Now I'm talking as if I was some sort of a psychologist. Ah, go figure!"

So what's the next step in trying to analyze this predicament we find ourselves in? "We're running out of ideas," and I'm getting a little tired of trying to entertain myself. Besides I don't know this park very well, and there was nonetheless anything within or outside these grounds I find myself in. "This whole thing is cloudy!"

"This bizarre obstructive sensorial in a physical sense" has my brain in an internal affect become unreliable. "Could this expose a disparity that infiltrates a quarrelsome dispute amongst myself?" Here I go again talking as if Mr. Psychiatrist showed up (uninvited).

After taking one more trip around the park to see if we could identify anything, I knew it was a waste of time. Has the allusiveness of my thoughts while sitting back on the bench help me any? "Well, we're back on the same bench." We woke up on this morning. Hopefully it will allow me to relax for I'm getting tired. I was aware that it was starting to get dark again, and I wasn't for sure of what to do next.

As I was watching this clogged up fountain trying to push water out of its nozzle, I started nodding off. So here I was lying down on this park bench, and after several hours of rest and sleep, I woke up, and I noticed the fountain trickling water alongside the spring running into the basin.

"The beautiful bushes and flowers were shining in such an exquisite array," and the walkway leading down to this central location was in cobblestone looking authentic as if you were over in a foreign land in the middle of a square. There I sat bent over with my head lying in my hands thinking, "Was this real or was I dreaming? All I know is that I'm happy to be back!"

Just a Little Spoonful

A STRANGE SENSATION started to brew one day when I saw a "spoonful of what looked like diamonds, or could it be gold staring at me in the face?" Or was this a spoonful of coffee, tea, or was it a special love that came my way but didn't realize? Could it be something precious that would satisfy my very soul? Upon looking at this site, it had me wondering how the vision came to be.

Yesterday I don't seem to remember how the seasons have changed that left me out in the cold. I was hoping that I would watch it shine with a pocket full of change or did we lose another day of sunshine?

From within, I kept asking to fill my hole with love saying, "The world is mine today!" There comes a time this was a dream for a tomorrow that we had wished for. Are we to see a few heads popping running their proposals of what their proposition would be? From a perspective view, one may wonder where has this image come from? Is it from you or me?

A taste of a premonition could permeate the aches of yesterday that allows a dismissal of someone's past. What will they say about this?

There came a time I thought we found someone, but there will always be exceptions. "I want you to know!"

Along the way, we saw empty faces lurking around with frowns as they seemed to be lost and somehow forgotten. "Confusion set on my face." What do I have to smile about now? This put a strain on my conscious; it left me perplexed. How do I get out of this puzzle? Would the fantasy leave me to be? Or did I somehow dream this all up?

As we pondered dancing around in circles, I wondered, "Is there a tune that would make us all happy or was I swimming in a pool with no water?" These delusional circumstances that keep roaming within the mind has a spark of their own.

At this moment, a woman came up to me and said, "Follow me. I have something that is good for you."

I inquired, "Who are you?"

Her reply came as a shock to me, but she said, "Sonny, I'm here to look out for you."

I was stunned by her answer, and then she gave me a "spoonful of medicated goo" and asked, "How do you feel?"

I was curious about what she had put in it, but was told it was her special recipe. She surprised me, but strangely enough, I did seem to feel better.

This lady told me, "Now you're ready to go on your 'merry ole way.'"

I respectively gave her my gratitude. I told her how thankful I was and started down this lonely street. While traveling on this hard-paved street along the way. I saw a dirt road that got my attention. As I stood there at the intersection, my curiosity had me talking to myself.

Glancing at the street sign, it had stamped on it: Withering Heights Drive. So here I find myself, standing at the crossroad, trying to decide which way should I go.

While walking in the direction of this gravel barren road, I found out why they called this "Withering Heights Drive." Around the first corner that we came upon, I saw these tall limbering willows and elm trees, and they were hanging over the street like a "wishbone from a spooky horror film!"

The sun was setting beyond the trees and hills, and there was no light from the stars or moon. This misty fog was floating inward toward the fields and trees heading my way. The skies with its rippling grayish cloud lines were announcing their stay!

While we were glaring at the sudden change, the noticeable temperature has dropped a few degrees bringing some cool breeze.

The road we were on has become as black as the night above; my thoughts had me wondering, "Did I go the wrong way?"

Swallowing my pride and suspicious mind while walking along this dark way, I kept my feet going forward hoping I would see some light. This darkness had me somewhat frighten. "Where will this lead me to? Hopefully to a place that I may know!"

Struggling as I was walking on this gravel road in this pitch-black night, I was thinking we must walk a mile or two, and that's when we saw a very dim light.

There was a small glimmer of sparkle shining through the trees that illuminated the sky. As we approached, getting a little closer from each step, I looked at it amazed. The light seemed to come from a shallow window in a small hut that glowed away.

I thought to myself that it was getting late, and I'm lucky to find this place. Let's stop by and ask for a little help to find out where we are at.

Approaching this place, I questioned myself, "Should I knock on the entry way or knock on the window?" But before I knew it, a little old lady met me at the door. Speaking to her, I asked her how she knew I was there. Her reply was that she saw me coming from a rather long distance.

I thought this was uncanny, where would this woman get her insight?

She was generous and had invited me to come inside and stay awhile. She also implied that she didn't get many visitors. My imagination started gazing at the idea how could she know I was coming in this dark night with no moon or stars shining their brightness along the terrain of such a wild countryside.

She made a comment to me, noticing I was in deep thought and asked, "How long have you been walking on this road?"

I told her, "Since this afternoon."

With a stern look on her face, she warned me if I did keep walking along this road, it will lead me nowhere. But if you don't adhere to what I'm saying, and you stay on the road, it will take me to dark and strange places, surprises, you will encounter wishing that you had never met.

After the sun goes down, and when it gets dark as it is tonight, the darkness seems to come to life, and these mysterious and uneventful things happen! She said, "I don't even go out at night. Too many unusual unseen sounds and voices you hear, that shouldn't be there! And speak about the darkness, it's so black you couldn't find your way around anyhow. Look out for those eyes at night. I see them amongst the trees."

But she said, "Never mind that now." Without another word, she offered me a spoonful of her own remedy. "This will give you insight on the right path you should take." She went on to say, "It will also give you strength to keep going forward."

I asked her why she wanted to help me, and she said, "Because I had a son, just like you from my past."

A Visit at the Lake

Stillness was sitting by itself during the night of day with lingering sadness for it was all alone. There was nothing around to bring it some hope. Bleakness seems to be forming within the edges of its domain, wondering, "Is this the way it's going to come?"

Would this relinquishing expression stay with me forever or do we have a chance to get away? How has something so unfortunate invite us in? Did we not see this coming our way? Or have we been traveling on the wrong road?

You were always so far away. Let's try not to run away like we always do. Walking alone on a path to nowhere, you approach the smoothness of a lake, and when you bent over to get a drink, you see a reflection of yourself. While looking at this face, you seemed to be talking to it! While talking to this vision in the lake of water, we asked, "Do you know where we need to go and what to do?"

This mental image with a smiling outlining face implied, "Be patient. There will be places to see and certain things you will run into." He told me to keep walking on the path I see!

Pondering on that statement had me a little puzzled, but when we glanced back in the lake, the vision I saw had disappeared! I questioned myself, "Did you just make this up? Or is this real?" My curiosity was going beyond me. I couldn't tell if he was right or was this just an illusion.

A picture of a sad notion was noticed while following the interpretations that were formed along the blades of grass. Has someone been wondering how this came about? A scratch from the earthly surface causes lines to show up! What a bumbling distortion was caught in its premier presentation, causing me to stumble amongst the rocks on the shore.

And when we fell to the ground, I got up on my hands and knees, and upon glaring up in the sky, it appeared someone has painted it blue with pink polka dots. My mind seemed to have lost control of what I'm looking at!

I feel as though I'm beside himself, or am I inside myself but lost in a maze?

"Hey, you got me all wrong, and now I'm worried." Where did this influence come from? It appeared there's something strong that keeps touching my face!

You find yourselves with glassy eyes while observing the strange surroundings we seem to be lost in. Rubbing your head with hands torn up allowed doubts to surface. With a confounded look on your face, you frown, wondering, "How did this happened?"

This mesmerizing thought from the past may be busted, but we can't seem to forget. You ask the winds, "Don't let my mind become post-toastee like I've seen a lot of my friends did!" Why can't we watch it shine asking the world to be mine for the day? Nonchalantly you find the path that's been in front of us all along. Will it wait for your response?

While strolling down this trail beside the shoreline, a glimpse of brightness was approaching, and it was so small; it was as if you were looking through a keyhole into another world. As we were closing in, this glowing ball was getting bigger and bigger; it seemed to be moving toward us.

And when it got so close, it began to sparkle before it vanished into thin air! We had our eyes covered when it flashed away. To my surprise, everything around seemed to be the same.

After turning around in a complete circle, we commenced on walking with a frightful sense of suspicion. When my conscious cleared up, we saw the glittering ripples guiding their way across the lake.

An illuminating reflection was dancing along the waters, following the haziness of rays coming from the sun. This shiny sensation had you swimming with the fish below as they were blowing kisses in the pool.

Finding myself casually walking on this sandy terrain, a voice seemed to be sadly talking to me in a manner that we had a hard time trying to understand!

There, the lake was speaking with sounds of crying, mumbling, "Where is everybody? Why don't they want to play with me anymore!" When we heard this, I stopped and glared at the waters by the shore, and there seemed to be tears flowing across the sands and rocks beside the grass.

As I bent down to touch the grass, a woman was standing behind me and asked, "Did you hear that too?"

With a sudden surprise, I turned to look and was astounded; she was standing there with long brown hair and eyes to match and seemed to have a concern look on her face.

I pondered while staring at her, and I finally replied back, "Who are you? And where did you come from?"

She hesitated, then responded, "My name is Francine, and I came over the hill and far away from the other side of the lake. Since we're introducing ourselves, what do they call you?"

"I'm Ethan." And then I asked her, "What did you hear?"

She thought about it for a second and said, "Sounded like someone crying, and I wondered who. Was it you, Ethan?"

"No, it wasn't me. It sounded as if it was coming from the water in the lake. But how could anybody believe me when I have a hard time believing it myself?"

Francine inquired, "Is that the reason why you were bent over feeling the wet grass and sand?"

"Well, at the time, I thought it was a good idea, but now I'm not for sure. It's just too high on the bank for the water to get it wet from the shores of the lake."

She implied, "What did the voice say? It wasn't too clear to me."

Scratching the side of my head to her request, I responded, "This is what I think it said, 'Nobody wants to play with the water in the lake!' I believe that's what it said, or I'm having delusions thinking I hear water talk?"

Francine had a curious expression on her face and made a staring suggestion, "We don't hear anything now, maybe it's time to go."

As we were leisurely strolling along the path, Francine started with some small talk. In a relaxed tone, she asked, "Where are you from? And what are you doing here at the lake?"

My curiosity had me wondering why she wanted to know about me. I decided to tell her, "I'm from Cold Stone Peak, and I came here to see the water and the liveliness that lives with the lake."

She smiled with those big brown eyes and began to giggle, "Well, did you see some life around the lake?"

I smiled back at her and asked, "What's so funny? I've seen more than my share."

That remark had Francine laughing a little louder. I couldn't quite figure out what she was laughing about, but I didn't say anything to her. I thought let Francine have her fun.

Her laughter had me somewhat intrigued. As I gingerly looked around trying not to be conspicuous, I did notice there wasn't much life at the lake. Puzzled by this, I thought who was fooling who!

There's something strange about this lake with water that talked and about the glowing ball speeding through the air and then disappearing in front of me! Now I don't see any life! With my imagination wondering, it came to mind that I had better keep my eyes open to see if we notice anything else unusual.

Walking amongst the pointed jagged rocks that formed along the trail had our feet aching from the sharpness that were sticking out of the ground. When we got across this part of the path, we needed to stop and sit down to rub the soreness that we endured.

We found a place to sit and proceeded to take our shoes off and started messaging our feet. When I got bold enough, I asked Francine, "Who did you come with? And how long will you be at the lake?"

Francine looked at me inquisitively and thought to herself, *Why is he asking me now?*

Pondering on the question, she responded unsure of herself, "Not until they come to pick me up, then I'll have to leave!"

I glazed at her with curiosity, but instead of trying to pursue it, I thought I'll leave it on that note. There was something unusual about the way she said it; that was what I was thinking. At least that's the way it came across to him. Then she asked me, "How far are you going? You do realize that this is a big lake?"

I replied, "I'm not for sure."

While all along we were walking, Francine announced, "I believe we'll be coming up to a steep ledge that we will have to cross."

As we approached, I glanced at it in awe! With a frightening look on my face, I said to Francine, "Is this the only way we can get over there?"

A smile was on her face, and she said. "Surprise!"

While we were following the edges along this steep path, a peculiar occurrence was arriving. Up ahead, a sudden darkness of clouds was drowning out any noises that might have been around! The silence that surrounded us seemed to be louder than our voices.

I noticed the clouds were rolled up like s scroll crossing the sky. Francine told me, "The ledge is slick. Do not lose your footing here. It's a little way down!"

I was stunned; there wasn't much room on the ledge, and everything around me seemed to get darker! We could only see about five feet in front of us. I had a worrisome thought in my head, *What if it starts to rain! That could leave us stuck on a narrow ledge afraid to move.*

It appeared when we first began to cross this slippery slope that we were thirty feet above the shore, where the water was slapping against the edges of rocks. And there was no other way to go.

I shouted out to Francine, "How much further do we need to go?"

Francine hollered back, "I believe we're getting close!"

By the time we got to the end of this narrow ledge, the darkness subsided and left us behind. The partly cloudy sky came in to take over. When I glanced at Francine to make sure she was all right, I commented, "Now that was a strange coincident."

But Francine leisurely acknowledged that's not unusual because it happened to her earlier when she went through it.

Now I had a look of shock on my face when Francine told me her story. My tone of voice sharpened, and my anger flared. "Why didn't you warn me earlier!"

With a stern look, she said, "I didn't know if it would happen again! I don't predict the weather! Besides you're the one who wanted to come out this far."

I began to rub my chin and started to apologize for jumping on her like I did and said I was sorry. "I had no right to act the way I did."

Francine noticed I was sincere and told me to not worry. "Apology accepted."

Then he suggested, "Let's sit down and take a break."

We were both getting somewhat thirsty with parched lips, and I mentioned, "Sure could use a drink of water about now. Guess we'll need to wait until we get down there by the lake."

After we rested, I asked, "Which way should we go, Francine?"

She suggested, "Let's just keep following the path, and there's a stream around the next bend."

As we were walking the trail, it began to decline to a steady slope. When we saw the corner of the lake, there was a small finger of water going inland.

With excitement, she shouted, "There's the stream with its cool and clear water."

When we reached the stream, she was right; it was delicious to drink, and it was so clear you could see the bottom with all its rocks and plant life. We decided to lay down beside the stream with our feet hanging in the water. The day was getting warmer when the clouds went by, and the sun was starting to shine.

I smiled with content and said to Francine, "Now this is the life, lying on a sandy shore with cool feet and a warm feeling touching your face."

While I glanced around, I noticed Francine, and she looked as though she fell asleep. That reminded me that I was tired myself. After a long nap, I woke up and found Francine gone. Looking attentively all around, I finally saw her swimming in the stream.

I shouted at her, "What are you doing out there?"

She answered back casually, "I'm getting cleaned up. They called on me it's time to leave."

I enjoyed the time we spent together; maybe we'll run into each other again. I cocked my head sideways, not realizing what she was talking about. Then I glanced around in circles and wondered who called her; there's nobody else here!

I hollered to Francine, "Who's picking you up?"

She looked at me thinking to herself, *He must be worried, and he doesn't understand.* She started walking across to the other side of the stream. While drying herself and putting her outer clothes back on, she shouted to me, "Don't worry. There're coming!"

While Francine was looking up into the air, a big clear bubble was drifting in. I was peering back and forth at Francine and this clear sphere that was moving toward them. I yelled to Francine and asked, "What is that?"

She replied, "Just wait and see!"

This translucent ball was gently floating and landed beside Francine! She waved to me and then proceeded to enter inside this frosted glass! As she was standing inside this transparent bubble, it started to float up in the air.

While idling in the air, it stood still and allowed Francine to wave her last goodbye. She was wearing a white satin lace dress with her diamond star halo floating above her head.

I waved back with a sorrowful look on my face.

At that moment, the bubble flashed with a bright sparkle and changed into a glowing ball that flew away into the sky! I was amazed at what I just saw and wondered if I would ever see Francine again.

Now it came back to me how it all began earlier in the day. I also noticed the abundance of life that seemed to suddenly reappear.

I thought to myself, *Somehow time must have changed or stopped while she was visiting the lake.*

Misty Dreams

THERE WAS ONCE we were strolling along that morning, one hot summer's day, when I laid myself down to rest in a big field of tall grass. I could feel the sun caressing my face, and we "fell asleep dreaming." "I dreamt" we were a star in a fanciful Broadway play, "which blew my mind." What would we be doing on stage of a glamorous play?

But there we were taken to a place, the hall of a mountain king, and I stood high on a mountaintop naked to the world in front of every kind of girl. There they were standing in many different shapes, sizes, and colors.

Out of the middle came, a lady, gibbering in a strange tone of voice and language. She whispered in my ear something crazy. She said, "Close your eyes. See the world!"

I pondered to myself and asked, *What could that mean?* I knew we were lying in a field of tall grass when the vision of the dream came upon me.

And again, she said, "Close your eyes. See the world.

When I looked around, she had disappeared! Now I could feel hot roaring flames running up my spine. A hot breath overcame me, and it seemed to have knocked me out upon viewing the horizon from the hillside seen earlier in the day.

This elusive motion that I saw earlier had me suspended in mid-air. I was wondering, *Could this dream be real? Or have I been shaken up seeing illusions that aren't even there?* A discourse of my eyes closed and the thoughts of visions were reappearing. There was an unusual gathering of people standing there watching me! Trying to understand a reason of what just happened had me thinking, *Am I still dreaming? Or are we on the edge of going crazy?*

Once again, she came up to me and said, "Close your eyes and see the world." Now I knew we weren't dreaming, but if it's not a dream, then what do I call it?

"A monarch of a transpiring orange-and-black-tip wing" flew past me in a hurry to a parlor to suckle the plants below to have a parley. This world I thought we knew has turned upside down; it was hard for us to recognize it anymore.

The "change of colors in my dream" had shown what they could have been. Enhancing the extremities of brightness allowed you to notice things are not the same! Who has ever seen the fields of "grasses become blue, the skies above green, the trees around are orange, and the ponds and lakes were red?" You would think you were in a land of a big candy cane, resembling a circus in a parade.

Looking surprised at an unusual but sensational delusion got me suspicious! I thought if we could only touch the grass and tree to see if it was real might answer some questions. Talking to myself, I asked, "Would the colors change and will we wake them up?" Neither transpired, instead we were amazed nothing happened! The colors of these sparkling exotic jewels fascinated me beyond the illusion of wonder.

Going along a path, I found myself following a beaming yellow light guiding me down a strange trail. On the way, we tripped over an orange branch, and we found ourselves face down amongst the purple rocks! Chuckling at myself for being so clumsy, I laughed.

After this awkward moment, we corresponded within oneself as we sat down on the yellow course looking and holding the purple rocks in our hands. I looked at my situation and found out I didn't even bruise my knee.

With a touch of sarcasm, I said to myself, "Okay, Lucky, take a breather, and we'll try again." Several minutes went by, "Well, Slick, are you ready? See if you can get back up on your own before you fall down again."

And we would repeat this funny gesture before we regained confidence, and in the meanwhile we were giggling about our circumstances.

Collecting my thoughts and putting them together as we stood back up, I noticed, "Am I on the wrong path?" The next thing we realized, something has changed. I found myself walking across a "floating mist of greenish smoke!" The lightness of its touch as if I was strolling along on fluffy feathers had me looking closely curiously down. It appears while walking upon this dust of an elusive delusion that the mist of this foggy smoke has vaporized some! Glancing at the bottoms below the coolness of the moisture was blowing into my face. I was in shock as we were crossing the skies above with no end in sight!

I started to recognize a confusion, which was rising in front of us. There was a serious dilemma I had to contend with! I questioned myself, "Where am I at? And how did we get here? And how will we get back down on the ground?" This unusual predicament, "walking and crossing the clouds" along a "misty fog," of an unknown substance has me bewildered to what my actions should be! While whispering underneath my breath, asking, "Where will this lead me too since I see nothing below or in front of me in this 'gloomy misty mirror?'"

At this time, I heard a voice behind me, and when we turned to look, this lady I'd seen earlier said, "Close your eyes. See the world,"

Upon closing my eyes, we were laying in a field of tall grass on a hot summer's day. A kiss on the cheek from a butterfly brought me back from this hallucinating dream.

Sitting on the Side of a Stone

In a serene area of a countryside setting while strolling beside a shallow creek bed, you find yourselves questioning or perhaps even challenging your own intellect. With a quaint smirk on your face, these thoughts seem to "pop up in your head without warning." You're conscious, without realizing it, "questions the mind!" You ask yourselves, there must be an answer coming along, but with doubts circling within the frame of your conscious, you challenge the response that you had received from earlier times.

But you say to yourselves, "I could have missed it," not knowing when I might have vanished from this lonely place of merrymaking. Have you fallen into a trance? Or is this merely a daydream that just happened? My thoughts kept asking me, "What are you doing? Come on your own. Leave everybody alone, for you find yourselves wasted, and you seemed to have lost your sense of direction."

In this delirious mind-set, a feeling of crying came over you today, but I promised myself I wouldn't do that again. Why should this voracious appetite keep taunting my desire?

Where has your self-control loom to? It's though it catches you off guard, waiting for the opportunity to "seize your weak soul" and then has the "audacity to laugh at you," thinking you have a good friend.

I've been staring at these empty pages of life. I kept asking myself, "Where? Where did all the answers go?" For there's nothing in there but blank paper. I pondered with dismay, "What am I making out to be in this weary atmosphere?" This shimmering flare that I had at one time has fizzled out to a no spark flame.

One day at the railroad depot, we were sitting outside the office on a wooden bench when I heard the teller calling to the passengers, "All aboard on the train to nowhere."

I asked the conductor, "Where is nowhere?"

He told me, "Don't worry if it passes you by, this train they're riding, does go nowhere."

A passenger that came off the train heard me and said, "Now, brother, don't ride this train. You will find it in vain, for it seems to blow its whistle, and when it runs around the bend, it ends up nowhere."

Scratching the side of my head, I pondered on his answer and asked, "What's the point of going?"

He told me, "People like to spin there wheels just as this train does too!"

Sometimes I see myself stuck wondering how some of these thoughts ever arrive to my brain. These imaginary ideas that seem to surface sure do befuddle one's inconspicuous thoughts. "Don't you say?"

This quaintness of normality that has the better of you seems to be the way to go, but when you find yourselves not paying much attention, the mind seems to wander around like your feet do. It seems I know what I want but can't quite reach it; the perils that block us won't allow you to feel what you've been missing all along.

"Oh my," the bridges we need to cross just to find your sanity, "to ask if it is all right," have you had questions about it before? Have you ever lost yourselves and afterward become dazed during the aberration of the day? "This coldness had you shaken and shivering beyond your sense of control." The shock took you beyond disbelief, stuttering to yourselves and questioning what has just transpired!

One day, we found ourselves standing alone by the highway looking for a ride. I waited a second hour; it seemed like forty days, and I thought at least we have no fare to pay. But after evaluating the circumstance, I had no ride neither. I questioned the motivation that put me in this unusual predicament.

"Of course, there was no answer either." While glancing upon the nearby dirt fields, I heard the wind whistling by to visit me. And as the voice was beginning to talk to me, it cried out to me and was asking, "Where are you going from here?"

I pondered about the question, but I didn't answer to the humming sound of swoosh. "It got tired of waiting on me," and it finally went away and left me in that field of dust.

As I was collecting my thoughts, I decided to put them in a box. I thought maybe someday when we need them, I could pull them out and use them to my own heart's desire. There is a possibility, even with my limited amount of knowledge, there's something we could use at a later time. I thought if not, chalk it up for hopeful exaggeration on my part, but surely there's something we can use! "I guess we all have the opportunity to dream at some point of time."

A staggering discovery came my way; we found our hope in a pleasant dream, and when my face lit up, it seemed to show a smile. But when it came to the end, I looked at what had happened with my head hung low.

I questioned it and asked, "Was it all worthwhile watching the gladness turn into sorrow and had lost all desire?"

Walking along a shoulder on the side of the street, "I saw pieces of an unforetold story." So I bent over to pick up the secrets that were laid out on the road. It was showing me places that I didn't understand or know!

"This shiny piece seemed to want to jump out of my fingers!" I was looking at it strangely holding it tightly, and it was acting as if I was invading it somehow or another. "I glared and questioned the fascinating pieces in my hands and asked, "Why don't you want to show me the secrets that I've been looking for?" While gathering my wits of what just happened, I glanced down to my hands, and when I gently open our hands, we didn't see anything there! "I was stunned. I know it was here for a time in my hands, for it seemed so real. Where have they all disappeared to?"

During this observation, my clarity seemed to be wandering, and it was unavoidable. My mind was just not making much sense. I couldn't get away from the sound that was shouting inside my head. There was something caught that could not get out. I was criticized of what went out, and when it came back in, I found out she was all right.

As I decided to walk alone, the lights were low. I didn't know where my life would go, whether emptying the shoebox or filling it up while crossing the snow. Rolling along the way, will I see a bitter end coming or should joy mysteriously jump out in front of my face, anxiously smiling at me?

There must be someone watching for they think I know what has been shown and what is hidden. I've been surrounded and accused of guessing the way it ought to stay; they forgot the fragrance that brings the pleasant smell into place.

Viewing a cascade of waterfalls heightened the exposure on the surface, and it intensified the feelings that were hidden from the blindness of one's eyes.

For your eyes seemed to look out forever after being brought forward from a "glass in the mirror." Were you still glancing and asking, "Is this just a make believe you happen to stumble on?"

Have you ever found the keys that can lead you through those doors that have you stuck in the middle of the floor, so it could bring you back from the distant past of antiquity? These thoughts kept pondering at us just from "sitting on a stone" beside a creek bed that keeps running into the river of dreams. Has my imagination taken me to places of the unknown, and I'm wondering, "Is any of this real?" Could you tell me when the clouds will clear from this foggy mist that has us secluded on the other side of a drawbridge that doesn't seem to work?

In this quiet blue background, draws out a response that seems to excite a slow reaction, allowing you to be a little more vivid with your tone of voice. Will this concentration relax the inner heart and soul? Or have you been hypnotized into thinking so?

A classical scene has sent you a view of a musical theme that has no sound. With a confounded disturb look, you question the melody, asking where the noise is. I see the instruments that are playing on the stage! So who's blowing the horns and where are the fingers stroking the strings? As you glance at this further, you questioned your hearing. With an angry voice, an answer was received. It said, "You have your earplugs in!"

So here I found myself sitting on a rooftop waiting for the "sky to cry." "I saw tears" forming along the edges of the mountain peaks, glaring its glassy eyes, looming alongside the turn of the horn.

When the sunshine came out, I saw a crowd sitting on benches and playing in the park grounds, holding flowers in their hands and growing them out of their hair. I saw ice cream stands with people in lines. It looked as if this was an ice cream social with people talking and laughing about the good time they were having. The children were playing on the swing sets, merry-go-round, and teeter-totters, laughing and making big rackets of shouts and screams.

They were asking, "Isn't it time for lunch? When are we getting our ice cream sandwich?"

An announcement was made saying, "As soon as you eat your sandwich, then you may have your dessert, and that will consist of an ice cream cone in various flavors."

Sitting and glancing, I noticed a pond with ducks and geese, so I went down to watch them swim and play. Being entertained from this sight, I decided to turn and look back at the park, but I saw everybody was gone!

I took a glimpse back and found the ducks and geese had fled away with the pond! I asked myself, "When did this happen? And where have they all disappeared too?"

In earlier days, when life was a little less complicated, it seemed to be more pleasant, but as time goes by, it seemed to hum along and dance. We seem to get a little dizzier having to come "eye to eye" with a foolish expression written all over your face. Is there any solution that may bring us out of this bizarre inclination? Or have we lost our path somewhere inside this road were on?

An unusual suppression may weaken and dismiss the reappearing of something that's not here!

Could we go about once again, for I have an important message to pass on to my brothers and sisters? Let them know I'll be all right, for I've been sitting on a stone waiting for a "blessing to come by my way." Hopefully this will "spark a brightness" that I may see one day.

Careless Direction

DURING A MIDNIGHT rendezvous, after visiting some friends, I decided it was time to head back home. While walking alone, I made a wrong turn. Instead of going right, I went left, in which I noticed and didn't catch myself until it was too late.

The night had a slight misty fog that was floating in the air, surrounding the street I came across, which showed something rare! After proceeding, it looked as though a streetlight was dancing with the reflection from the full moon that was on displayed. There were streams of light rays spraying from the streetlamp, and it acted as if there was a party, but I didn't hear a sound. I knew the streetlamp was getting excited because it kept on buzzing; flashes of light were turning on and off upon the constant glow of its partner's dim brightness.

While glancing at this for a minute or so, I thought to myself, *It looks as though they're having fun. Well, it's time to move on.* At that moment, I was thinking with some perplexity to get back on track. I will need to circle the blocks so I can head for the right direction toward home. I determined to myself I would save some time if we just kept the course were on. So I gathered myself together, and I looked ahead to see how far the next streetlight was. As I was walking down this street somehow, I noticed that the road was getting narrower, and the streetlamps seemed to be farther apart from each other than what they had been!

Well, it appears I have entered the beginning of an alley. I was walking by trash cans and dumpsters on the rear sides of these tall buildings, where I saw fire escape stairways. While still walking toward the next lamp stand and glancing at the backside of these buildings, my curiosity asked me, "Where are the door and window lights? I didn't see any!" And I thought, *Thank goodness for the full moon.*

As I was approaching this streetlamp, I heard noises as if there was a big hoop-hoorah going on.

My subtle mind started to get more anxious. When I got closer, I witnessed another sight. There was a dog, cat, and a mouse talking to each other. I happened to overhear their conversation. At that moment, George the Cat asked Ralph, "How about let's go dancing?"

Ralph the Dog said, "Okay, let me ask Stanley."

He said to Stanley the Mouse, "How does dancing sound to you?"

He said, "Great!"

As they were jumping around in circles, they proceeded to get on their hind legs dancing under the street lamp, and they looked as though they were wearing tutus. They were dancing as if they were ballerinas with their paws together over their heads in a ballroom. I didn't know what they were trying to do, but they were having fun.

I heard the dog howling, cat purring, and the mouse chirping from smiles on their faces as if they had finished a steak dinner. I couldn't help it but started giggling inside and asked myself, "What are these idiots doing wearing those skirts? Well," I told myself, "we had our entertainment for the day. It's time to keep going if I'm going to make it home before dawn."

Starting to walk again, I thought I was on the last leg of this long three-block alley, and when I came up to the next streetlamp, I saw two guys in raggedy clothes, and one of them had a hat on. The one with the lighter clothes on was moving about; he was taking his hands and patting his arms and shoulders as if he was trying to stay warm. At times, he would put his hands over the lit fire. They were both huddled and would walk around this lit trash barrel for heat. They had their hands over the fire. I thought they must be hobos living on the street.

As they were talking with each other, it was hard for me to understand what they were saying; the only exception was I heard one call the other one Freddie. So I got a little closer, and I stood still in the shadow. I noticed they were sharing a bottle. It looked as if it was wine. The one with the hat blurred out, "Lenny, I wish you would stop whining about the cold and sit still. It's not even that cold yet."

"But, Freddie, I don't have as big a coat as you do. Let me wear it for a while."

Freddie barked out, "Lenny, go find your own coat. I'm not going to shiver like you are. Besides you left yours at the last place we were at, and some other bum stole it from you."

While they were still arguing, I happen to see two large cardboard boxes against the building wall, and I thought that must be there sleeping quarters. The one in the hat, I found out between the two talking, was Freddie, and he also had the bigger coat. Now that makes the other one's name Lenny, and he asked Freddie, "How about we cook up the rest of that gumbo. I'm getting hungry."

Freddie replied, "You must have a hollow leg, Lenny. Every time I turn around, you're always hungry again. Well, go ahead and heat it up on our high-dollar stove before you get spasms."

Lenny turned back around and said, "Thanks, Freddie."

While Lenny was heating the pot over the fire in the trash barrel, he asked, "What are we going to do tomorrow, Freddie? We won't have any more food left."

Freddie shrugged his head and said, "I must need my head examined to put up with you." He shouted to Lenny and said, "Tell me something I don't know."

He told him, "We'll just have to hit the restaurants, and we'll start at Pearls Place and mosey on down to Rolf's Diner, and hopefully we'll find some breakfast or lunch. If things get worse, we may be able to eat at the mission if we didn't use up all the free passes we had this week. And we might get a free shower to boot."

As I had enough of their tenure for the day, it was time to walk away. As I started to pass them, they saw me and looked at me somewhat surprised, wondering where I came from. But they didn't do anything, and likewise on my part, I didn't say anything either. I just kept walking, and in about five minutes, I reached the main street. It was good to be on a familiar street again. This turned out to be a better show than what I've seen on television. I looked back and said, "Goodbye and good luck."

Wishing Wells from Tomorrow

ONE TIME IN the early cold morning, while listening to the tunes on a radio, I heard a song singing, "Wishing you were here." It kept repeating the quote, "wishing you were here." The soft voice relaxed me so much I started thinking I was there. This wishing of today seemed to have my attention and made me wonder "why should I be in a place I don't know."

As we were casually lying down, my impression found myself in this picture of a streetcar rushing up the road to a destination that was unknown. As I glanced down from the ceiling in the room where I was staying and watching myself dozing off, sleeping with my eyelids flinching with little spasms, I inquired to my mind, "How did this come about?" Then I saw myself rushing through the wall floating in the clouds to a place I haven't seen before. The next thing I realized I was riding in a bus, or was it a train? I couldn't tell. I heard someone shout next, "Stop!" When the conductor stopped the car, I scrambled up to the windows to see where we were going! Running down the street, along the way, we would hear a bell ring before it completely stopped. And after a few stops, I finally saw a street sign. It read, "Michigan Ave. and E. Grand." I asked, "Where is that at?"

A man standing amongst the crowd heard me and answered me by saying, "We are going downtown. Don't you know where you are?"

This unusual circumstance had me questioning myself, "How did I get here? And where is it taking me?" I asked a lady standing beside me while she was holding on to the standing pole and tossing her handbag from one shoulder to the next and said, "Where are we going?"

She commented, "Silly, we're going downtown."

I looked stunned at her and said, "What direction is that?"

She told me, "East to the heart of the city."

These huge buildings and structures outside the car made me wonder, "Did I really wish I was here?" The presence of all these people baffled me; they were stuffed like sardines in a can; and I didn't see any smile on their faces either.

As we focused on the strange faces that were coming and going, I noticed everybody seemed to be in a hurry. Rubbing my stubby chin from a lack of a shave, I pondered to myself, "What is the big rush all about?"

Will they see something special that they don't want to skip? Or do you have an appointment you can't miss? While speeding down this concrete pavement, I heard someone shout; hurry to the conductor, for I'm running late.

Somebody else spoke up to say, "Do not worry about this car, Old Desire, will get us there on time. She's been running down this line for ten years."

A woman started telling the people around her that, "Old Desire has been so faithful to us, and we're proud of her. She makes sure you get to your destination on time. Even the conductor that drives her makes sure she gets all the attention she needs during her garage inspection because she's been such a good gal."

This car speeding down the road infatuated me. How could these people love this streetcar so much as if it was their kin? I took the liberty to step up to this woman and asked if I could get a cigarette from her. She smiled at me and told me, "I don't smoke, but if you were to ask that gentleman over there, he smokes."

With a reply back, I said, "Thank you."

I nudged my way up to the gentleman and asked if he had a spare cigarette we could get from him. He took out his pack and said, "Here, have one."

With a reply back, I said, "Thanks."

He told me, "No problem, but don't make it a habit of borrowing them."

My unconscious reaction grabbed one and lit it up puffing, blowing ring clouds in the air. While I was calming down, we were beginning to try to understand how we got there that might make some sense of what we are doing here. As we were traveling along this street, I noticed and observed these bigger buildings that were reaching for the sky. It was hard to see the sun peeking through the clouds as it was trying to bring a little sunshine to the place. Gathering the few brain cells I had left, we realized this wasn't a delusion from a dream. "We were really there," but I still marveled, how we got here. "And where is here!"

As some of the crowd were leaving, new passengers were boarding so they may reach their destination, wherever it may be inside the city. I heard some conversations people were talking about how they were dreading work and wished the day was over, and they were on their way back home. Others were discussing what their plans were after work, whether it was eating dinner at some high-dollar restaurant or going on a shopping spree. Still others were saying, "I'm so broke. I'll be lucky to afford the streetcar to work next week."

But most of the passengers inside had long faces, staring along the walls and out the windows from the streetcar they were in. There was this old man I happen to catch a glimpse of; he happens to find a seat to sit on, and he kind of made me laugh as he was shaking his head from side to side while rolling his eyes at all the complaints that people were making. As I was squeezing myself through this pickle jar, I happened to be stuck in; we managed to get close enough to talk to this old man.

With humor, I asked him, "How are you doing young, man?"

He looked back at me with a small grin on his face and replied, "At least you're a polite youngster, or are you trying to have some fun?"

"No, just being a little respectable to my elders."

"Well, I can tell, you didn't grow up around here."

I asked him, "Where is here?"

He glared at me puzzled about what I just asked him. He told me, "You're in the windy city."

"Oh, is that the reason why most people look so glum?"

"Na, a lot of these city slicker folks are nothing but a bunch of simpletons or wannabes."

As I started giggling on his comment, I told him, "I've noticed you've been having some fun with these passengers."

"Yea, it helps pass the time, besides some of their issues they bring upon themselves, that's how smart they really are. So," he asked me, "if you're not from around here, what brought you into town?"

"Well, it started on a lazy day while I was listening to some tunes on the radio, and I heard this relaxing song singing, 'Wishing you were here,' and I must have dozed off sleeping, and I landed here."

He studied me from head to toe and said, "Well, it doesn't appear that you've been hallucinating." Then he inquired, "You didn't break out of the funny farm, did you?" He looked at me with a funny gesture on his face and said, "If you don't belong around here, then where do you live?"

I told him, "I'm from the hills outside the city. I'm waiting for a clue to lead me back to where I came from."

He told me, "Well, good luck on your venture. I hope it works out for you."

I stared with a deep look in his eyes and said, "Thanks, me too."

At that moment, I heard the whistle blow. They let me off the streetcar and told me I was on my way back.

A Picnic of Dreams

WHILE CASUALLY WALKING, a curved path was approaching, and there were a few twists that seemed to get in the way, and Seth shouted, "How far are we going in? We could have stopped and set up about a hundred foot back."

Jody brought up the point that, "The girls need to find us, and they're bringing food too."

Between the two announcements had Alex thinking, and he replied, "Let's stop and set up the barbeque pit back there."

They all thought that was a good place because there were some big oak trees and a nice spot for the sun to peek through, and the makings of a barbeque pit with partial stones already exist. When they started unloading their backpacks and dropped the ice coolers beside the firepit, Alex asked, "How far are we in?" For this was a narrow-wooded section with a dirt passage that led you into the thick part of the forest. When Jody and Seth heard Alex, they both looked at each other, and after their leisurely debate, they agreed they were about one hundred yards in the woods, the same length as a football field.

There was already a single border of rock around the firepit, and we brought two grates with us to cook on. These wire grates were about sixteen inches in square, and we had them wired together and tied off to one of the backpacks. Ingenious don't you think? Anyway that's what Seth told Jody. Jody shrugged his head at Seth and replied, "Oh yea, just the cat's meow," with a tone of sarcasm in his voice. Alex just stood there with a big grin on his face and thought, *We're sure getting started with a big bang.*

Still chuckling from the humor, Alex suggested, "Well, one of you guys get some firewood and the other get some kindling to start the fire, and I'm going to find some more rocks. We need to raise this up for the grates to sit on and have enough room to keep the wood underneath and try keeping our food from touching the ashes."

They all agreed on the chores we needed to do. Alex persuaded them, "Before we get started, let's have a beer first."

They laughed with amusement and shouted, "Let the games begin." As the three of them were drinking, Seth informed Alex that he had seen some rocks about seventy-five feet back and off to the left. While we were coming in, Alex made the comment, "Well, that will be the direction I'll be going toward." Then he smiled and invited them to help, "If you guys see some rocks, will you bring them back?"

No problem was there answer. And they both looked at each other thinking, "Yea right!" After finishing their beer, they separated and went on their own merry way. Alex crossed the path of where they were at; he headed down along trying to find the rocks, and within a few minutes, he was starting to get a little disappointed. He didn't see much but brush and trees as he was following the dirt path to what he thought was nowhere. He glanced to the side, and then suddenly he ran into the area where the rock pile was.

Showing some enthusiasm, he began to appreciate the stockpiles of rock just sitting there for the taking. Alex started looking for the flattest rocks he could find and began a pile off to the side, so he could gather them up when he had enough to carry. He thought, *If I could stack them in a formation that we could carry, we could do this in one trip.*

As Alex was filing his arms up with as many rocks that he could carry, he heard a noise in the woods! It sounded like a chuckling from someone, and the other sound sounded like a friend murmuring saying, "Look at this guy. He's stealing jewels from us again."

And the other one said, "There will be a price to pay."

And Alex shouted to the voice in the woods and asked, "Who are you guys?"

The petrified voice said, "We are the gatekeepers of the woods."

And they hollered, "Why are you taking our rocks?"

And Alex told them, "I'm just borrowing them."

Then silence preceded; it had him wondering as he looked around, and he didn't see anybody but trees and some rocks, baffled with a disturbed frown on his face asking to himself, *Who was I just talking too?* So he shouted out and asked, "Would it be okay to borrow some rocks?" And he saw two huge oak trees; it was as if the bark was lifted from their eyes and mouth!

Alex was stunned when he saw the eyes were in front and back, and his mouth opened in a jaunty hue, enabling a refreshing smell as if it was lime, sparkling a glistening of perfect perfume. The trees spoke amongst themselves and thought it will be all right as long as they don't leave the woods!

When Alex reached down to pick up the rocks to hold in his arms, the vision he saw with the trees was gone!

Alex, when proceeding to walk back to camp bewildered, talking to himself, asking, "Was what I saw real?" His demeanor was unaccounted for; his train of thought has lost its compass. He began wondering in his demoralized slim brain, *What have I just seen!* When he got back with the armful of rocks there was Jody and Seth drinking a beer waiting on Alex, and they asked, "Where have you been?"

Alex told them; it took a little longer than anticipated, and he didn't dare tell them what he had heard or seen.

Alex was slowly stacking the rocks around the firepit and blurred out, "This will be ready to light off in a minute." His thoughts were still wrapped around the experience that he had with the trees. At that moment, Jody handed him a beer while Seth was preparing the kindling in the middle of the pit. As he got it lit, he started adding little more, gradually feeding the fire in the pit.

The appearance of his facial expression shown to Jody had him somewhat concern, asking if everything's all right. Alex sitting on a cooler of iced-down beer and food pondered on the speculation, maybe he was being too obvious. He just shrugged it off telling Jody he was just glad that he could relax again, thinking let the good times roll. But down deep, he was contemplating, wondering if it was just his imagination!

When Seth sat down next to the firepit and was drinking his beer, Alex got up to move, for the cooler was starting to bite his cheeks in, and he chuckled at the idea of his ass hurting, and there was an old stump sitting there with a big patch of grass growing around it, and thought I'll just park it there. While moving, Jody was sitting on top of a log and was drinking beer faster than he could blink his eyes. Before Alex could sit down and get situated, he heard another can, pop open.

While the two of them were jabbering to each other, Alex caught a glimpse of the fire, and while it was heating up, he noticed the shattering rocks jumping and scattering as it turned and burned; his eyes happened to see the rocks asking to the cold flashes, "Where are you hiding yourselves?" It looked as if the small flames were dancing on the logs trying to reach the end as they looked for a chance to jump off and cool down.

As Alex was thinking to himself, he mentioned to Jody, Can you throw me another can of beer because I think it's time for a little more help?

The three of them were chiming in just as fast as they could swallow, and after the third one, it seemed things started to calm down a little. While we were laughing and reminiscing about the past, Seth glanced at his watch and mumbled, "Where are the girls at? It's twelve o'clock!"

Jody reminded Seth, "I told them we would hang a red ribbon on the trees by the path and thought that would be okay."

But Seth wasn't happy' and insisted, "I'll wait another five minutes. If they're not here, I'm going back to see what's going on."

Jody and Alex replied, "Whatever you think, Mama Hen," and started smirking. The five minutes have past. Seth got up and started muttering where could they be, heading toward the trail and told the other two, "See you later."

Staring back at the fire in the pit, Alex looked at the woodpile and suggested to Jody, "We should get some wood so we won't run out later." He glared at the situation and thought that it might be a good idea, then he made the snide remark, "That's what happens with old dried-up wood. It burns to fast. I'll go get some more," as he shook his head somewhat disappointed.

While the two were gone, Alex started glancing at the fire again as he was adding some more wood to it. At that time when sitting back, he saw the sparks flying in the air like flies hovering around an old watermelon. As he was watching it, it seemed he could feel this fervent heat attaching itself to the flint while it was crying from the spark that's been following its trail.

Still glancing at the fire, Alex was looking at the small rocks popping in the air, and his thoughts took him to a journey imagining the sounds it was making were the sounds of someone making popcorn. He heard noises coming up the path, and Seth was helping the girls out by carrying a cooler of wine and ice. They had two small coolers, and the other one had potato salad, beans, coleslaw with some paper plates, cups, and buns. Alex made the mistake of asking them how their trip was. And Wendy barked out, "Okay, just okay until Sandy and Carol went ahead and dropped and spilled the cooler of ice and wine."

Alex with a sheepish grin on his face implored, "Well, at least you were lucky it was the cooler with the wine and not the food."

Carol reputed me and said, "What's funny? Anyway we had lost half of our ice."

Then Wendy was complaining who was the idiot that wanted to have a barbeque out this far, and Sandy along with Carol both chimed in agreeing.

Jody showed up about that time with an armful of wood and made the comment that "this should last awhile."

After bringing up the complaining again and on other issues with it also, the guys got tired of listening to them and told them, "Just chill out and have some wine. We thought if you're going to run your mouth, maybe you should put some wine in there too."

They thought—well, now taking it a little offensively and looking at them with scornful bold eyes—they thought, "Oh no." Then they in turn said, "That sounds better than running our mouths all day." While they looked at each other, they thought, "Why not?" They looked at them and said, "Amen!"

The guys kind of glared at each other and thought, "We just got away with that one."

As they were sitting around the campfire, split up in two groups, the girls over there and the guys here, they noticed the day was still young as they were gossiping to one another and each having their own drinks. It sounded as if the girls were starting to have some fun as they were laughing and carrying on while reaching in to grab another wine cooler.

Now Carol was talking to Seth, her boyfriend, about getting her headlights fixed and said, "When are you going to help me?"

Alex happened to overhear and asked Carol, "What's wrong with them?"

She answered back, "They don't come on all the time. They'll blink or flicker from time to time."

So Alex replied, "Well, let me see them, and I might be able to help."

Carol said, "You can't see them now!"

Alex asked, "Why not? All you have to do is lift up your shirt, and I'll examine them."

Carol looked at Alex and shouted, "Not these, you imbecile, the ones on my car."

Alex looked at her with a dumb look on his face. Then Carol turned her head to Seth while he was shaking his head from side to side; she gave him a rather dirty look and said, "Well, are you going to say something or just sit there looking stupid?"

He mentioned to her, "Well, honey, you did kind of fell in that one."

Then Carol glanced at Wendy. "What are you going to do with that man?"

She coolly said, "I don't know. I haven't figure that one out yet. When you come up with any good ideas, let me know."

Jody and Sandy were giggling about all this, then Sandy told Carol, "Don't worry. I think Alex is jealous you got something he wants, and he can't have them."

At that moment, Wendy smiled and said, "Go with that girl."

Well, Carol and Seth decided to go out into the woods. They guessed for a little makeup discussion. Jody suggested to Sandy still giggling and said, "Let's take a walk ourselves," while each one had a beverage in their hands. Some disappointment seemed to be the expression on Wendy's face when she said, "I'll be back in a little while after you've had some time to think about it." Before she left, she looked at Alex and muttered, "I hope you had a good time on that stunt."

Alex came back and chuckled, "Doesn't she have a sense of humor? Besides I thought it was getting a little boring." Alex stared back at the fire thinking, "I'm all alone." Well, he thought, *Maybe I deserve it.* Gingerly reaching for another beer, he was aware of the excitement continuing as he sensed something strange was going to happen! His eyes felt funny, and they got to twitching, and he stood there exasperated as his mind started flinching and seeing flashbacks of something that occurred years ago. Then his memory imagined he once saw someone running in circles with their head lying on the ground. He thought, *Did I just see someone without their head on their shoulders! It must have been something out of a movie!* He stopped himself just in time to watch the smoke rising from the fire on the pit. It seemed as if there was a separation. The movement started wiggling, and the vision looked exotic while it was introducing you to a trance. This form of a spiral dance had him, wondering, *Was I being hypnotized?* And that's when he heard *clip-pity-clap* sounds as if they were coming from small hand cymbals.

Alex imagined, "Is there a gypsy girl dancing around in circles within the smoke in the air?" About that time, there was a big poof, and the scene was gone! Gathering the pieces of his mind, he was trying to put this confusion back together. Alex found himself sitting in front of the fire, hearing the crackling of wood while burning. He looked around and was still all alone.

Astonished on the circumstances about what happened at the fire, a conversation came up as he was talking to the woods, a feeling got him looking down as he found his feet were walking. Stunned he wondered, "Where is this going?"

Upon entering an open field, a fixation of the light he was following showed white clouds moving smoothly along the faded-blue sky. As the sun was peeking, Alex saw two-eyes piercing through the sky glancing side to side as the clouds were floating by. Then the two eyes slid back from where they came from. When he glared at the clouds again, he saw what looked like a pink tongue splitting the sky and taking half of the clouds with it when it went back in to hide.

About then, Jody and Sandy came up and glanced in the sky with Alex and asked, "What are you staring at?"

He quickly turned to them and answered, "Oh, it's just you guys."

They glared at him with a puzzled stare and said, "Yea, what were you looking at in the sky?"

He told them he wasn't for sure! Jody suggested, "Since it's about two o' clock, let's start cooking."

And then Wendy showed up and overheard thinking, "That sounds like a good idea. I'm famished, and I'm sure everybody is getting hungry too."

Alex just stood still, still gazing at the sky waiting for something else to happen!

* * * * * *

Sandy mentioned she would help, and they all walked back to the coolers and the firepit. Alex was following, and he proceeded to get another beer and asked Jody if he needed one. Jody laughed and said, "I've already got one," and he began stoking the fire to a higher gleam while he put the grates on the rocks. Now Sandy and Wendy were opening the packages and preparing the food that needed to be cooked.

There were hot dogs, hamburgers, and chicken with two cans of large pork and beans. Carol and Seth came back and offered to help, and Jody said, "Wash your hands and make up some burgers." He asked Wendy and Sandy for the chicken first and gave him a bottle of barbeque sauce while they're at it. It looked as though Jody was running the show on the grill, and Wendy was attending to the beans and had them ready in a pot. The guys had a special way of preparing the burgers; they would mix ketchup, A.1. Sauce, and habanera sauce in their right quantities and mix the ingredients with the hamburger.

It seemed to give them better flavor; plus, they say they won't fall apart on the grill.

In about an hour, the chicken was starting to smell good, and Jody signaled to Seth for the burgers. Now Sandy jumped in and said, "I'll bring you the burgers. Remember I'm your helper."

Jody apologized and asked, "Sandy, could you bring me those two platters of burgers."

She replied, "You bet, sweet thang you."

Everyone around started laughing about that insinuation, and Sandy suggested, "I think we found his new nickname, didn't we, sweet thang?"

Jody looked at Sandy and said, "Now look at what you just started pudding pie, now we all were giggling."

It seemed that Sandy hit a button, and she knew it.

While the burgers were sizzling, and the chicken were on the cool end of the grill that Jody asked, "Okay, whoever give me the hot dogs and lay them on the grill there."

So Sandy took the wieners out of the packages and dumped them on the grill. Jody just took another sip from his beer and kind of gave her a disgruntled look as he started straightened the hot dogs out.

Carol motioned to Wendy, "Would you help me and we'll bring the rest of the food out?"

She inquired, "Where do you want to put it?"

Carol answered back, suggesting, "We could put the two coolers together and use them as a tabletop. We can set the plates, bowls, utensils, and anything else for serving."

Wendy thought, "That will work, and it will be our little buffet," as she smirked about the very idea.

About twenty minutes went by, and Jody announced that lunch is served, and we all said, "Thanks, sweet thang you!" While they were all filling up their plates and bowls and began eating, Alex was just standing by, and Wendy turned her head and said, "Grab a plate. It's ready."

Wendy asked, "What have you been doing all day? I haven't seen you very much!"

With a distant stare, it seemed he was not here. Then he made a rather unusual statement, "I must have been dreaming lying under that big tree that's been talking to me, showing things that I wouldn't have believed."

As he kept standing there, Wendy looked at Alex kind of funny and asked, "Would you like me to bring you a plate?"

He said, "That would be nice."

When Alex received the plate of food, he heard others talking about their day's events. As Alex began to eat and had two bites before silence had gathered around, and when he looked up, there was nobody to be found! What happened? Where did it go? And when he looked down at the plate he had had disappeared! After glaring at the place he was at, he pondered, *This isn't even the campsite we were eating at!* Alex found himself talking to the space that surrounded him and wondered, *How did this come to be? Has my weariness got the better of me?* He went from talking to walking, and that's when a big black bird flew by and landed on his shoulders. Alex was stunned, and he warned him. "What do you want with me? And don't you dare put your claws in my skin!"

He looked at Alex, twitching his head from side to side, seeing if he could find a better view! While glancing at him, Alex asked, "Are you a raven or a crow?"

He glimpsed at me and said, "What's the difference between the two?"

Alex told him, "They say the raven is bigger with a longer slender beak and has luxurious shiny black feathers."

He quickly answered, "Well, that's what I am then."

"What's your name, raven?"

He answered back with great excitement, "They call me Archibald the Bold. What do they call you, stranger?"

Alex mildly grinned and said, "I'm Alex the Great," trying to tease this bird and not diminish my caricature.

At this moment, he flew off his shoulder and settled on a stump and asked, "What brings you here?"

Alex perplexed about this whole thing implored, "Where is here?"

The raven responded, "Here is Here!"

Struggling on what he just said, Alex questioned his own doubtfulness. He couldn't recall or know what brought him to this place!

He cackled with a loud shrill and laughed from his expression and said, "You'll find out! Nobody comes visit us unless they've been invited."

Alex questioned, "How will I know this?"

"When he's ready to see you, he will let you know."

And Alex inquired to Archibald who he is.

"He is He. Don't you know anything?"

"So what do you do around this place?"

He proudly admonished his usefulness. He stated, "I've been chosen as the greeter of newcomers, and I will also announce you when the time is right."

Alex was astonished. "Announcement for what?"

He said, "As being our guest for a short while! For we don't get many visitors in our land of Forevermore!"

Alex was baffled. Just simply puzzled, he asked, "Why would he want to see me?"

"Evidently he has his reasons, but for the most part, it must be something important for he told me to be humble and charming!"

Now Archibald had Alex wondering, so he had to ask, "How long have you been here?"

The raven replied, "As long as I can remember!"

While walking around admiring the scenery, Alex noticed the raven was getting somewhat curious and asked, "What are you looking for?"

"Nothing out of the ordinary, just enjoying the silence of the trees and landscape while viewing the splendor of the sky above with all its beautiful clouds."

Not understanding Alex's notion of appreciation, the raven cocked his head and moving it all about, stomping his claw feet in the stump. Alex couldn't help himself but giggle over his ridiculous action he was performing. Then Alex had the audacity to ask him with a humorous smile on his face, "Is this a new dance? And could you teach me?"

Archibald rambled, "Very funny. You're the one who seems to cackle like a mother hen trying to find her chicks."

Alex said, "Touché. You do have a sense of humor."

While gabbing with the raven, a ruffling breeze was blown through the trees awakening them up from their slumber! The clouds were running across the sky as quickly as possible to get away from the darkness that's been following behind them! The wind began to whistle so loudly Alex had to cover his ears, even the trees were bent over so slightly that he could hear creaking. He saw the raven was hiding with both wings covering his head!

The next thing Alex realized, the wind had subsided, but there was a cyclone of twirling wind spinning so fast he could barely catch his breath!

Then Archibald announced to him, "This is Alex the great, and this is He."

Alex asked He while he was circling around like a whirlwind that's been riding a tornado, "Why have you asked me here? I don't remember coming to this place."

He answered and said, "I wanted to personally thank you of your hospitality for showing respect in my land." He also added, "Do not tell others what you have seen and heard."

Alex bowed with courtesy and said, "Thank you, sir."

He told Archibald, "You may give him the gift now."

The raven flew up to Alex and landed on his shoulders, and he had a shiny transparent green stone in his beak. He told me, "Hold out your hand. This is yours from us."

As soon as the raven dropped the stone in Alex's hand, he was back at the campsite with a plate of food in his hands. Wendy told him, "You better start eating before it gets cold."

Alex asked himself, "Was that real?" And when he checked his pockets, there was a shiny transparent green stone he found.

Walking the Rail

WHILE WALKING DOWN the railroad tracks heading for the next small town, a flourishing flock of geese flew over me, squawking away at the new sky. The time of day showed it was about nine o'clock according to the sun as it began to heat things up. Traveling along this rail about a mile or two ahead, I saw something approaching me, and when it got closer, I noticed it was a dog wagging his tail as he came up to me. Staring at him, he looked kind of skittish. He said hello in his own style, looking at me as if he needed a friend. As we glared at each other for a minute or two, I told him, "You're welcome to come along. I could use some company." it seemed to put a smile on his face.

While we were walking, I happen to glimpse at him and noticed he was trying to keep his paws on the wooden ties. I guess it was cooler than the rocks in between. Talking to this dog and glancing at this four-legged creature from time to time had me curious. "What's your name?" I asked.

He stared at me and was tilting his head from side to side, not understanding a word I just said.

But he did figure one thing—I was talking to him. Scratching my head and pondering on the question, I just asked how can he tell me his name when he can't even talk! "What are you thinking about?"

He did have a small white ring around one eye and looked kind of rugged, so I thought I'll call him Blitz. Besides he was a short stocky fella, and with that name, it made me laugh.

Walking along this barren track, we must've went about four or more miles, and it was time to take a break. We saw a tall shady tree off to the right, so we stopped to sit there awhile. The heat was getting quite muggy and humid; this was a good time to shed some more clothes and put it in my backpack. Blitz glimpsed at me with his tongue hanging out of his mouth, slobbering, trying to get cool down.

Sitting under this tree, I brought out my canteen and had a swallow of water, and this dog sat in front of me and gave me this look that said, "How about me?" Well, I looked for an empty container to put some water in but didn't find one. So I decided to use the palms of my hands so he could lap whatever I could hold. Of course, neither one of us seemed to get a whole lot of water, but at least we got our tongues wet.

As I commenced to drying my hands off using a bandana, a thought came across me. Well, let me roll up one of those cheap cigarettes; it might be a long time before I have another one. While smoking and glaring at this dog, a question popped into my head, wondering what kind of breed he is. Focusing on this medium-size brown mutt with white socks and sad eyes. With a white ring around one eye stunned me; this is the first time I really paid much attention to him.

While staring at him, he smiled showing his teeth as his tongue was hanging off to the side like he was trying to get his wind back. I giggled at him and said, "Yeah, I agree it's going to get a little warm today."

After our rest, I stood up and took my knapsack and canteen. I put them over my shoulders and looked at the dog. "Are you coming with me? It's time to go." As we were on the tracks, glancing at him, he was sitting beside the rail and looking straight ahead into the brushy field.

As I was walking the line, I happened to glimpse around, and there was no dog. So when I turned to look behind, he was still sitting on the side of the railroad tracks, staring right at me. Wondering to myself while glaring at him, I asked, "Are you going to come or stay?"

He just looked at me with a glaze. I thought he will have to figure this one out for himself because I don't know what he wants or where he came from. About fifteen minutes went by, when I turned to see where the dog may be and saw a small image on the side of the tracks and thought, *Well, I guess he made his choice.* Thinking to myself, I was just starting to get use to him being around. I'll miss him. I went a little further up the tracks, and when I glanced back again, the blurriness of the heat waves off the rails had me kind of blind; it caught me by surprise. I was curious, wondering if that could have been a hawk. Pondering about this had me thinking, for at that time, something went up into the air, and it flew away. I anxiously looked back down on the rail, and the image was gone! I had a suspicious look on my face, asking myself, "What did I just see?"

With the sun over my head, I could tell the day was getting warmer, and it must have been past noon. My stomach started growling, and I thought as soon as I get around this curve that's up ahead, I'll stop to take a break and eat. While walking, I ran up to a black snake crossing the tracks. It looked as though there was about two feet hanging over each side of the rails, where this snake was making its route. There it was about twenty-five feet away as I stopped and waited for this snake to cross. He didn't bother me, and I left him alone also. It only took about five minutes, and he was off the tracks heading for the bushes to probably find a place to cool down.

As I started putting one foot in front of the other, ten minutes must've passed by, and I was coming up to the bend. When approaching this curve, about one thousand feet in front of me, there seemed to be a bridge.

When I walked up there, there was a trestle going across a steep ravine where there was a creek with big rocks running through it. Looking up and down this steep creek bed, there was no good place to cross within eyesight. Staring at the rail and wooden ties, they appeared a little shaky, and when I tested the bridge, I felt the crosstie was slightly losing its grip with the rails. The length of this trestle was about a hundred-foot long and probably seventy-feet plus down.

A decision had to be made whether I should eat here or try to cross then eat. I chose the latter. This shaky trestle made of steel and wood had me thinking twice. I'll sit over here and rest, then it will be time to go. In the meantime, I took out my tobacco pouch and rolled up a poor man's cigarette to smoke and calm down.

A black cat came out of nowhere and curiously gazed at me, then proceeded to walk across this bridge on the rails. As the black cat reached the other side, she turned back and said *meow*. Then she sat down staring like she was waiting for me. I thought, "What a show-off. Well, she made it look easy enough. I guess it's my turn now!"

Getting ready, I strolled up to the trestle at the edge of the bank while looking at it closely. I told myself, "There's no way I'll be able to balance on the rail like that cat did. First, it's semi-curved, and it's not wide enough! Let me see the condition of the wooden ties." Noticing some cracks and splits, they were spread out about distance of twenty-four inches apart. Between the ties, you could see the creek and rock bottoms, which gave me the jitters just from looking at it. When I finally got the guts with my head on straight, I slowly put my foot on the first tie and heard loud squeaking and popping, then we just went for it.

Walking the ties with a fast but steady pace, there were some strange noises. By the time I got to midpoint, I happened to get a quick glimpse and noticed the black cat was licking its paws one at a time. I thought, "How casual you can get!"

While stretching my legs from one cross tie to the next, I got myself in a hurry before reaching the other side. I was a couple of ties away when suddenly a movement on the trestle began. At that moment, I jumped to get off and landed on the other side. Astonished by what just happened next took the wind out of my sails. When I looked back, most of the wooden supports and beams just split and collapsed!

As part of it fell, the echoes coming from the banging sounds sure got my attention as the stone piers were crushed, and all the debris landed against the rocks and creek beds. When the dust settled, the pieces of splinter wood and girder beams were just crumbled up with rails on top. I could tell from age that this trestle has not been used for a very long time.

Initially the black cat jumped straight up into the air from the noises and startled her just as much as it did me. When we both glanced over the bank of the ravine, we saw piles of rubble fragments that were damming up the creek. When I got my clarity back, allowing me to relax, I thought how lucky I was that nothing happened to me. As I sat there, I commenced to rolling up a cigarette and had a drink of water, sitting there staring at me was the black cat. After this bizarre incident, I managed to reflect back to where I was, and I heard my stomach starting to growl again.

Rummaging through the knapsack, we found a can of Beanie Weenies and peaches and decided this was lunch. While eating out of the can, the black cat came up to me purring. I knew she was trying to make friends with me when she smelled the wieners from the can. So I gave her a half of one, and to my surprise, she ate it. Well, I ended up giving her the other half, while I had the rest. When the peaches were gone, it was time to get going again if I'm going to make it to the next town before the sun goes down.

The black cat was beside me while traveling along this straight track as we were both watching the sun drop further in the sky. It appeared to be about four o'clock in the afternoon. After going through that escapade earlier, I wondered how much further it was before I get there. During this casual lighthearted walk, we watched the sun drop about another inch at least from my viewpoint. I figured we must have traveled about two miles when the landscape had changed from brushy bushes and trees to open fields of different kinds of grass and weeds. Before entering the flat plains, there was a reflection from the sun standing upright toward the sky.

While walking toward the glare, several times I would see a sparkle twitching, and it would glimpse at the sunrays flowing from the heat. When we got closer, it appeared to be a silver-colored metal post. Of course, the black cat got there before I did. It turned out to be an old railroad crossing with a road going through the tracks and rails. Also, a sign with the X-brand design with the writings railroad crossing and the sign with all the bullet holes read, "Warning."

Talking to the cat, I mentioned, "How about we have a short break because I'm getting tired, and we need some rest?" Looking at my canteen, it was half full, so I had a swallow and brought out the empty Beanie Weenies can that I kept and gave some to the cat. She managed to drink most of it before she had enough, then the cat roamed around studying the area she was at.

Surprised by the sudden coolness of the wind as the clouds started covering the sky had me debating to myself whether I should put some more clothes on! Then the clouds rolled by, and sun was peeking out again, so I decided to wait, for it felt just about right. Staring along the tracks, it was time to get up on my feet, and when I glared ahead, it looked like some road tracks were off to the side.

There on the side of the railroad tracks were two old bare grooves going parallel with each other. I started talking out loud, thinking the cat would listen to me when I suggested, "This looks like they were used by the railroad, tractors, and their trucks." It was brought to my attention, the fifteen minutes we were here, I didn't see or hear anything along this road. I thought about walking on that old dirt road, but it was built up with so many high weeds and grass that I didn't want to fight them. So we decided to stay on the tracks. It was higher, and I had a better view of our surroundings. Struggling along the ties that were running opposite of the rails seemed to open my eyes, paying more attention to how I was walking. For I found myself staggering and almost tripping, having a harder time lifting my feet to the next tie.

While forcing my movement along the tracks, we started running into the thorny bushes and trees, and from a distance, we saw a huge hill forming up in front of us. As we got closer, the hill was gigantic, and there in front was a dark hole that resembled a passage to go through. At least that's where the tracks led you!

The black cat got to the entrance of the hole through the ground before me, and she started pacing back and forth in front of the cave. She would, from time to time, stop and gaze at me waiting for me to begin the journey through the passage. Looking at the cat then the tunnel, I saw a glimmer of light at the far end, which had me pondering with curiosity. Lingering about I was trying to figure out how long this tunnel could be!

Then I went back outside and had this strange idea about going over and across the top of this overpass. But when I examined the landscape and the thickness of thorny bushes and brush around, it kind of made me lose any enthusiasm I might have had. Well, as I was staring at the sky, deciding what to do, I asked the cat, "Which way would you go?"

She started walking back and forth in front of the tunnel again. I tarried around a little longer and thought, well, she gave me an answer. I noticed the tip of the sun was the only part above ground, and I knew it was going to sink fast. At that point, the day was getting cooler, so I began to put the clothes back on that were in the backpack.

When the black cat gazed at me with those big eyes, I said, "Well, buddy, are you ready?" And we proceeded walking inside a dark hole. When we got so far in the glimmer from the other end was getting grayer and dimmer than before, it dawned on me the sun must be down.

Every so often, I would strike a match to see where I was going. Something unusual was happening as we were approaching closer to the other end, the brighter the exit was getting! As we finally reached the other end, I looked out, and it seemed to be daylight, and when I glanced around, there was no black cat! When I turned around, the tunnel was dark. As I turned toward the front, there was a glaring brightness that I couldn't see pass!

Standing in the dawn of heat, a sizzle shaken with a glowing light brought forth a reflection of her flaming gaze. Along the colors arranged in different shades sparked a smile with eyes to match, and the twinkle from her dimples danced as if it was blowing kisses in the air!

The brightness had me turn around, for my eyes lit up, feeling they were burning up with desire inside my head. Rubbing my eyes, I turned to look again. This person I saw had a shine crossing her face, and she was wearing a yellow raincoat with yellow shoes and a standard rain hat. She also had a white umbrella while standing in the rain, and she asked me if I had the time of day.

I replied and said, "I don't even own a watch." Then I asked her, "Who are you?"

She said, "I'm an illusion that came out of your head. Why don't you recognize me?" Then she asked, "Where are you going?"

I told her, "To the next town."

Then she said, "Why?"

"I haven't found what I'm looking for."

And she asked, "What is that?"

I answered back saying, "I'm not for sure exactly."

Then she reminded me, "Well, it's time you go back to sleep, for I need to go!"

The next thing I remember when my eyes opened, it was daytime with the sun glistening over the horizon. I walked out of the tunnel, and the town was a little way down the hill, and the black cat looked puzzled at me and said *meow*. Astounded, I glared at the town, and I realized this was the place I was going to yesterday. Then I wondered, *Was all I saw just a dream?*

Glassman Smiles

UPON ENTERING THE house, Ho Hum and Zipples were talking about their little escapade while shopping earlier in the day. They were discussing how their day was window shopping in the mall and looking at different items in the stores. Overall they seemed very excited!

There seemed to be many interesting gifts, but what stood out was what they particularly found in the knickknack shop that sold many unusual glass figures, some with costumes on them for show.

They told Rudy what really caught their eye was what they seemed to think was a leprechaun. Ho Hum and Zipples were both trying to persuade Rudy to go down there with them to the store and get his opinion on what he thought about this little glassman. He said, "Well, I got some time. Let's go and see what's all the big commotion about."

When they reached the store, he noticed they had a huge selection of different types of glass figurines in assorted shapes and sizes. Rudy noticed this little man after Zipples pointed it out to him; he had a stocking cap and suspenders made of glass with his pants down showing his smiley ass, his knickers strap must've broke. Anyway Ho Hum asked him, saying, "Rudy, what do you think? Isn't he cute?"

When Rudy looked at this glassman, he thought he'd seen him grin. When Ho Hum said that, and of course Zipples was chiming in. But he thought, "I must be mistaken. How could a piece of glass smile!"

Zipples asked Rudy, "What do you think, Rudy? Don't you think he's a bargain? He only cost 149.95."

Ho Hum agreed with Zipples and said, "We even have a place picked out for him at home."

He replied to both of them, "Why ask me? I think you guys have already made your minds up, besides I feel like a sounding board, just so you can hear me say okay."

Ho Hum inquired to Zipples, "Well, we got the green light. I say let's go for it."

Rudy commented, "Before we buy him, let's talk to the store woman over there and get her opinion about this little glassman."

They both were excited and agreed on talking with the lady. They asked the woman about this ornament, and she said, "He is an 'elf and was blown and made in Brittany,' and the reason why I remembered is because he intrigued me. There's something about his face! He stands fourteen inches high and painted in exquisite array of colors that shines in the sun and glows at night. He's made of borosilicate colored glass. His name is Paddy Maloney. Why do you ask? Do you like him for he's a strange little fellow? He has an inscription on him that says, 'over the hills and far away!' He will also smile, grin, or show no emotion depending on how the light hits him."

She told us, "That's all I know about this glassman, and now I'll leave you alone and go about my business, unless you have any other questions."

Rudy glanced at Ho Hum and Zipples, and they both just kind of shrugged their heads no. The woman left them. Now Ho Hum and Zipples were just fascinated by this glassman; it was as if the little fellow hypnotized them into liking him!

So they bought him; there was no way of getting out of this one that Rudy knew of. When they got home, they sat him on the kitchen table admiring him for a little while, discussing where they are going to put him. They asked Rudy, "Do you think he would fit into our scheme? I believe we have a place to put him."

And silly Rudy thought, they already told him that they had a place to put him when they were at the store. So he said, "I don't know. He looks devious and shrewd with that mischief grin on his face as if he was waiting for something."

Ho Hum replied, "Oh, you're exaggerating. What do you think, Zipples? Is he going? [Six-o-one] looney tunes on us?" Zipples seemed to think they were both on their way to la-la land.

At that time, Rudy noticed that "Paddy the Elf smiled!" When he turned him around, he saw no facial emotion at all. It was if he was hiding an expression.

Ho Hum and Zipples were asking, "What are you doing to poor little Paddy?"

Rudy told them, "I caught him smiling!"

They looked at him and said, "He's not smiling. It must be all in your head."

He wondered how ridiculous this must look about a glass elf standing with a grin. Rudy asked, "Ho Hum and Zipples, where are you going to put him?"

"We thought by the bookshelves beside the back door on top of this nightstand," Zipples replied.

Ho Hum agreed and said, "That would be a nice place for Paddy Maloney, where he can get some fresh air and sunshine.

Rudy told them they were treating this little glassman as if he was real. "I'm surprised you didn't try to feed him some stew."

At that remark, it looked as though he was grinning on my comment, and Ho Hum implied, "Get real. We know he can't eat."

Zipples suggested in a laughing way, "I think Rudy is getting jealous of Paddy. We must be giving him too much attention." She giggled along with Ho Hum.

"Well, I didn't think he was the envious type, being resentful about a little glass elf who has a hard time keeping his pants up."

Rudy told himself, "I've had enough of this. I'm leaving the room and take a break from this hostile environment."

That just made the two of them laugh even louder.

After about fifteen or twenty minutes went by was when Rudy decided to come back into the room, and he noticed Ho Hum and Zipples holding the glassman like a baby and stroking his hair and arms and talking to Paddy as if he understood them. Between the two, they were showing their appreciation of how much they cared.

He also noticed a big smile on Paddy's face. And the two were taking turns holding and cuddling him as if he was a baby.

Rudy thought, "What a joke! He's got them eating out of his hands." And he stared at them and mentioned, "Do you realize what you're doing? Or is it all going over your heads? Paddy's got you guys buffaloed. He could lead you like sheep going to slaughter, and you wouldn't be the wiser! You're acting as if you were a couple of buffoons that lost their red nose! Wake up! He's got you under his spell!"

Now Paddy quit smiling; no emotion was on his face.

Ho Hum and Zipples stood up and put Paddy back on the stand and commenced to glancing at Rudy then at Paddy. And Ho Hum said, "Nobody has nobody." And Zipples followed suit denying any delusion on their part!

This little glass elf and his illusions reminded Ho Hum and Zipples that something was kind of queer about some of the events up to this point. They were talking amongst themselves when Rudy brought up and said, "This mischievous little prankster is playing on your mind, misleading you on purpose to hopefully get the better from you. He's a trickster that's his nature and somehow he's alive, he's living, and it appears he knows everything that's going on around him."

Rudy motioned to Ho Hum and Zipples, "Come over here by me," and he whispered in their ears and said, "Let's go into the other room."

Ho Hum blurted out, "What are we going to do with him?"

Zipples said, "Well, we need to get rid of him before he gets his own way! Anybody have any suggestions?"

There's something funny going on here with Paddy, the glassman that doesn't set right with me, and frankly I don't like it, it's kind of creepy too!

Rudy reminded them, "Take him back to the shop where you got him from and get your money back on return or trade him for some other gift."

Zipples was thinking, "What if they won't take him back, and we can't exchange him either, then what?"

"If they don't take him back, then drop him from the tallest building you can find and let him shatter all over the concrete!"

They all laughed about the gesture and said, "Sounds like a good idea. Then we can hear a bang!"

There and Back Again

WHILE LOOKING ALONG an unconcern scene, wondering amongst the sky and woods in a backward sort of way, promoted an unusual discovery. An image appeared showing its disarray of something that I thought was out of the blue. I pondered staring at it in several different views.

The climax had me puzzled. I had to ask who are you and where did you come from.

He said with a thunderous voice, "Do you not recognize me from the stars above with my shiny coat glowing in the wind from yesterday?"

I asked with humbleness, "What are you doing here? And why have you come in such a suspicious unannounced way?"

"I came here because we observed you from a distance just moving about in a boring way, talking to yourselves underneath the open sky. Besides you're looking for someone to talk to who has an open mind that can relate to you."

A delusional contemplation entered into my mind, *Why would he come all this way just to talk to me?* In my simple form of understanding, what does he have to say? Then I had to turn and glance away to see if this was all a dream, but when I turned back around, he was still there! His appearance stood out with a glow on his face, fire in his eyes, and his hair was as "white as snow!" Has one come out that's known the benefits of the unknown. It was as if he had me suspended in midair.

After retrieving my senses and thoughts, I took it upon myself to ask, "What do you want with me?"

He handed me these pages and said read, "Them yourselves?"

While looking down at these blank sheets, I wanted to know if there was a predication that may come my way, and would it comfort me finding myself observing these empty pages. I kind of felt dazed and confused, where are the written words that I should see on the page!

Gathering my recollection, I looked up and noticed the person standing in front of me, just smiled, and gave me a friendly gesture. I found my head spinning all around as I was trying to focus myself in getting back to normality. This realization of what has just transpired had my eyes rolling. Then with concern, he glared at me and said, "Are you okay? Looks like you have lost your self-control.

Has your common sense come back yet, do you know where you're at! Or should we give ourselves a break? I pondered on the suggestion that he made and had no objection.

With astonishment, I looked at him and said, "What were on those empty pages?" They seemed to put me in a delirious frame and had my head swimming, not knowing where I was at. Following his unique discussion had me bewildered about what he was talking about.

He noticed my thoughts and answered me, "Would you like to see the stars, the moon, and part of the universe?"

After grasping for air, I looked and asked, "Where are we going?"

He stared and said, "Just follow me."

Upon ascending to the clouds above, I noticed the wind caught me in a crossfire in which I couldn't catch my breath! He told me, "Do not worry. It will be all right when we reach the illusion that's shown on the screen."

My scrupulous curiosity led my mind to a bizarre delusion that got me thinking, "Who is he that says nothing is wrong! While venturing above the sky and clouds these bluish stars showed a sparkle that came our way, glowing a gleam of light that was too hot to touch or too bright to get up close." This enlightenment was a sight one could not look upon without glancing away from the brightness that formed from the rays that shined on your face. The strange impression I got was like looking upon forty thousand headsman coming my way, sailing across the seas, seeing if they could "change the course of my mind!"

As we were flying through the stars, my guide asked, "Would you like to visit the moon, for it's on our way to see more that's in store for us in the galaxy?"

I found myself whistling by the stars with such great pace that my "eyes were stretched back!" When we approached the atmosphere of this yellowish celestial body, we stood hovering in the air as if we were floating in a calm sea. As the moon was getting its brightness from the reflection from the sun, you could see the deep dimples that were formed upon its surface. I asked my host what caused these deep pockets to form on the moon.

He looked at me with his fiery eyes and told of a story about meteorite showers that come by once in a blue moon. When it happens, they come with such a powerful force, speeding through space looking for its own destination!

I was amazed to see how it could be exposing itself as a far distance land, wondering if anybody would ever come around. Watching this phenomena, we noticed there was no life or anything moving along this lonely surface. An unusual observation made an assumption, "Why does this place exist! Is it because it gives light to other forms during the night? My teacher says you're partly right. It also helps us to tell time with its different shapes. We will not get into that for its time consuming, and there are more things to look at. There is a riddle one may quote, 'day by day by neon light. It caught me two for two, eye for eye caught in a whirlwind where I couldn't catch my breath trying to reach my shadow asking, 'Where are we at!'"

I was astounded by this reaction that came my way, visualizing a creation that comes to the place I was standing about. About this time, another showed up. He must have been a friend, and they were talking to each other, and I couldn't hear what they were saying. Besides they were talking beyond my comprehension, and I didn't understand. Their language seemed to be above my level.

During their conversation, they agreed on something, and the visitor turned around and "suddenly disappeared!" I questioned him saying, "What was that all about?"

He said, "Don't worry. It's not important."

A dizzy feeling within had me asking; I've already seen more than what my eyes can hold. Somehow he read my thoughts, and with a smile on his glowing face, he reminded me, "We are just getting started. The journey we have in mind will be visions that you will not forget, for we have a long way to go."

My suspicious curiosity told me to ask, "Where are we going on another flight? And if we do, where are you taking me too?"

"Well," he replied, "We are going to visit the outskirts along the outer edges of this orbit."

I asked, "What does that mean?"

He smiled and said, "You'll find out what some may call the ghost of the skies!"

With a presumptuous look on my face, I asked, "Do they wear white sheets?"

"No, but they are a flashy white color!" He mentioned, "They are small particles and gases that have collected together, and their blazing speed travels amongst the stars and skies."

When we reached close enough to the sun, I noticed this bright ball heading toward the sun, and when it encircled the glowing heat, it came back around, and "I saw a very long vaporizing tail!"

With my mouth open in awe, I looked at him and said, "What was that?"

He replied back, "That appeared to be 'a comet,' looking for its state of hibernation, for it rests and stays inactive for many, many years if it can get away from the sun."

As my guide inquired, "It's time to go." And he told me to hang on. "We're going to fly with speed to another place toward the dark zone!"

While traveling in the dark, we saw cosmic rays heading for the earth's atmosphere before we flew in the opposite direction. He told me, "Do not be alarmed. They'll need to try to penetrate through the upper atmosphere before they can shower the earth with its tiny nuclear particles. And they will become so small that there will be little or no damage caused from them."

I thought how convincing that sounds! When we got closer, there were still some flashes of rays and cosmic disarray continuing ever showing the flames that it displayed. I've never seen a sparkle and glow that didn't slow down. This excitement had me wondering, *Is this pleasing to the eyes or is fear setting in? Will this ever calm down?*

I asked my host, "What will become of this? Am I safe?"

He said, "Don't worry. You're with me. This is only a premier of what will come next."

My suspicious imagination came again. "What are you talking about!"

While he had a grin on his face, he said, "It's time to visit the black region of a celestial body that enjoys swallowing things up. But don't worry, I'm here to prevent that from happening. Think of me as your guide and protector."

I looked at him and said, "Why would we be glaring at this if it can swallow us up?"

"It's part of the universe," was his comment!

While viewing this from the side and at a safe distance, I observed a bright extraordinary multicolored ring, and in the center was this big black hole. Witnessing the things that got to close in front of this big black hole, its gravitational pull seemed to eat different size objects up. I was dismayed!

My host told me that it also swallows light! In my imagination, I wondered and asked, "What is the purpose of this hole?"

He replied, "There are some things that need to go to another dimension where they will be more stable. If this didn't exist, we might have a cantankerous world where some may not recognize."

I was perplexed about these visual sights, and they had me in suspense. My mind seemed to get somewhat delusional to where I couldn't keep going. I said to him, "I think I've had enough."

He suggested, "Do you not want to see the meteors that fall like shooting stars going toward the atmosphere wondering if they will make it through like a rainbow from a lightning storm? Or would you like to see the little asteroids running around the planets showing their rays of light and the quickness of their speed going from here to there?"

I pondered at his generosity and said, "I think my head has been spinning since we started this sightseeing."

He smile and told me to not worry. "I'll take you back home. We'll go there another time when you're ready."

Section 3

Suspense Inside a Window

Hidden Behind a Door

A UNIQUE BUT disturbing notion entered my mind during an early morning sunrise. A premonition, perhaps an abrupt feeling of something strange was going to happen. It turned out to be a typical weekend morning, and by the time the afternoon came and went was when I received a phone call. A couple of friends called to invite me to come over and have dinner with them, and we'll play some cards afterward.

They jokily said no charge. I said, "Okay, I'm not doing anything special. I'll try to make it since it's for free," and started laughing. When I was ready to go, I left the apartment and began that early evening walking up the street. When I realized this was a little longer than what I anticipated. I looked earlier at the address; it suggested it was about ten blocks away. I've been having some problems with my car, so I thought a little walk shouldn't hurt me, besides my therapeutic self-counseling talked me into doing just that.

While walking up this street, I didn't know what would be ahead, but I did seem to see things a little bit more vivid than what I've seen before.

Half way, I started to get a little thirsty and decided to enter this building. It was a hotel "called the Silent Canary," which I thought was an odd name. Looking for a soda or a drinking fountain, "I noticed some doors around and down the hallway. I saw a soda machine. Digging in my pockets, I finally found some change and put this in the older type soda machine, but nothing came out. I tried again; still nothing happened. It stole my money! I told myself, "That does it. Where's the clerk at?" And that's when I realized as I was walking back up the hallway, I didn't see a welcome counter or anything else but doors.

I thought, "Let's get out of here. It's not worth it, but all the doors looked the same!"

While looking at these doors, they appeared as if they were built for a rich man's mansion. With eloquent brass trim and the hardwood looked as though it was white oak, shining as if it wanted to glow in the night. "Polished doorknobs which looked like gold?"

And when I glanced at the room, all the walls and doors were symmetrically in the same shape and pattern. I thought, "How unusual. Now this? I didn't notice upon entry into this place. It's as though I'm in another room!"

As I pondered, I thought I'll pick a door I think I came through. There were only twenty doors to choose from! I questioned myself, "What direction did I come through as I was glancing and searching for the door?" Standing in front of a door, I wondered, "Could this be the one I entered when I came through?" Then I got to thinking, I don't have any idea, for I didn't pay much attention of what transpired.

Looking closer, I thought it was from this direction. After searching, I picked three possibilities. I had this weird thought that crossed my mind, "Would I have to play this 'eenie meenie miney moe' game to pick out a door?"

The first door I gazed at, it looked at me as if it was saying, "Pick me, pick me!" So I reached for the door handle and turned it slightly open and started with a step forward, but I felt nothing below my foot! I began to slip into the room, and my foot was dangling in air as my hand held firmly on the door handle! Grabbing the handle with my other hand as I was hanging on the door. I managed to scramble back to the room I was in. The room was pitch-black, so I brought my foot back in a hurry and thought I'll lead with the other foot. Very gently and slowly, I proceeded. Still nothing there. "This eerie feeling of an empty space in the floor had me spooked!" I tried to reach my hand around to locate a light switch so I could turn the light on but didn't find one!

Curiosity had me in suspense to a point that I had to know and see what I might be dealing with! I decided to be a little more practical on my assessment! There seemed to be no floor. When looking down, it was as gloomy as the darkness at midnight! I took and threw a coin from my pocket inside the room, and we didn't hear anything until a few moments later, and it sounded as if there was an "echo that ringed from below!"

This was peculiar. "How far is the floor down inside the room? Or does it lead you to a place of the unknown? I stood at the edge of the floor, stunned, while hanging on the door. This certainly isn't the way I came in. Let's try another door, for I need to get out of here!"

Speculating had me quivering. If there wasn't a floor as it appears, where does it lead you too? My imagination was exploding with possibilities that took me beyond a gruesome horror!

When I closed the first door, I stood in front of the second door and cracked it open. I watched out for the floor. But instead of the floor, it was dimly lighted and what I saw were mirrors standing on different styles of frames in the middle of/on the walls and even the ceilings of this big room.

They were everywhere. I stood there amazed, thinking I could get lost looking at myself trying to get through the "reflections from all these mirrors." I even felt lost hanging on the door!

I kept gazing at these "mirrors" as if they could tell me which way I should go. Constantly looking at these shiny glowing images that was flowing in so many directions started getting me shaky and confused! My eyes seemed to be stuck on these mirrors. I had to try to diverge myself from this, but it grabbed me, held me as if we were being influenced by some hypnotic trance! I found that we couldn't move, being immobilized from the threat of these sparkling objects was submitting to your very mind, "put chills running up your spine!" My hand was stuck to the doorknob. Arms were frozen; I couldn't even cover my eyes!

As my mind came back to some reality, I decided to "close my eyes." I thought if I couldn't see this, it might not affect me and let me lose from the grip it had, squeezing its submissive bondage that firmly enclosed me. While keeping my eyes closed, my mind seemed to clear up some. Standing in the doorway with my hand on the door knob, I stepped back, and I closed the door. Upon closing this door, I realized we could have been locked in that room of torture!

A frightening thought crossed my mind, standing there wondering what door to try next! I was still dazed from the reaction of the last door. My imagination was taunting me, saying, "You're not dreaming! Grab another door handle. They're made of precious gold, so what are you waiting for?" I began shaking with a whisper in my head that made my heart thump a little louder! I glared around the room and saw a haziness floating and settling in the air. The doors were disappearing behind the cloudy mist! This urging feeling told me to pick another door for there isn't much time left.

Nervousness took over. As I reached for another doorknob, anxiety was developing within my emotions. Tension was grabbling my senses, realizing I had to open it up! Suddenly I twinged as if there was a striking pain. I was terrified of the response that may come forth while my hand was trembling on the handle! Very, very cautiously, ever so slightly, I turned the handle slowly, ever so slowly as my heart started throbbing, throbbing a little faster on each motion made, dreading what could be behind that door!

I cracked the door open wide enough to stick my head inside. I noticed the lights were bright, and the room was full of more doors that looked the same. With the door fully opened, I glanced around, and I counted twenty doors in this room. Same pattern, same shape, same everything!

Standing at the entrance of the doorway, gazing in both directions, I felt lost. Which way should I go? Now an eerie feeling came over me. Well, will I ever get pass these doors? I told myself, "Relax. Let your mind relax, just relax! Don't let this torment you! Just think clearly and relax." And after relaxing, somewhat I decided not to go in that room and start all over again. These doors were playing games, trying to trick me. It seemed to enjoy my fear as if it was looking at me and laughing! This hotel with these rooms and doors, there must be a way out, I kept telling myself. Without it, I would probably lose my sanity! I closed the door to that room I had just seen.

Standing with a frightened stare on my face trying to recover from these last three doors, I frowned about "the fourth door!" I kept telling myself, "Maybe we'll have better luck on this next door." These were the first three doors I picked out when I first started. And none of them could help me! When I was ready to turn the door handle, I thought, "I'll use my foot to open it up some."

When the door was fully opened, there seemed to be a big party in this private resort, people drinking and laughing while they were telling jokes. Upon glaring at this somewhat happy occasion, a man came up to me and asked, "Do you have reservations, sir?"

Glancing around, I noticed the men had different styles of tuxedos and the women wearing these eloquent formal silk and satin gowns and dresses. I realized I must be out of place. There was the sound of an orchestra band in the background and a dance floor off to the left side of the room with beautiful crystallized chandeliers hanging from the ceilings, and the walls were covered with passionate tapestries. I informed him that I was not dressed for this, and I must have lost my reservation. But he reminded me it would be. "Okay, sir, I can give you a tie and jacket that you may borrow."

When I mentioned my reservation, he told me to not worry; they wouldn't mind. He reached behind the bar counter and handed me a tie and jacket and asked, "Will this do, sir?"

I replied and said, "Thank you. That will be fine." I asked, "What do they call you?"

He answered back and said, "I'm Fritz, the doorman, sir."

"Who are all these people standing at the bar and others playing billiards? And what is the celebration all about?"

He thought for a second or two and implied back, "Well, these are producers, directors, and movie stars, and they are enjoying each other's company on the latest film. We needed to go a little further."

I asked Fritz, "Who is giving the party? And to who has the honor?"

He told me, "The actress Veronica LeBeau won the best actress award. With the director, Fredrick Von Hassen, so there is a party to commemorate their outstanding performance."

Surely, I didn't want to feel like an idiot out of place, but I had to ask, "Fritz, what year is this, for I think we could have lost a year?"

He gave me a rather odd look and replied, "Of course, this is 1937, for this is the time when we will bring the country back together once again. For everything seems to be on our side."

I thought to myself, *How did I get here!*

Fritz offered me a glass of champagne from the bar and said, "Enjoy yourselves, sir, and have a good time."

Before Fritz could walk away, I asked, "Have you seen the other doors?"

His response was, "What other door, sir? We only have three, one to enter the room and one for each facility." Then he said, "Would there be anything else, sir?"

"No, that's all, Fritz, and thank you."

While talking with a few people, the champagne was starting to go down a little easier, and as Fritz pointed out, we were having a good time. They all seemed to be pleasant in a sort of harmonizing way, talking as if things will be on the rise for an exciting new year.

As we were drinking like fish that wanted more water, they continued to laugh and tell jokes while flirting with each and one another. I must have gotten smashed; I woke up with my head on the bar, and when we looked around, everybody I met was gone.

My surprise of thirty-seven wasn't much different from what I seen in eighty-seven, fifty years apart, except the clothes and their attire. Well, I thought, small world. I shrugged my aching head, "Well, I guess I missed the dinner engagement that was set up last night." And as I was getting up, I managed to leave the room, looking around. There were three doors and a check in counter with an old man saying, "I trust you had a good stay?"

I asked, "Where's the exit door?"

He said, "Right through that door, sir." He also reminded me to have a good day. "It was nice having you."

Outside Looking In

GAZING AT THE misty darkness of night as lights were flickering from above, had you glaring, as you were strolling all alone on a crooked trail.

While looking at the show we found ourselves stumbling and fell in a hole. When we finally got to our feet we glanced around only to discover and ask, *where did we fall into?*

Astound by a hollow stone creek, as you heard a trickling sound of water coming from it. Alongside this creek bed a narrow passage was formed that led further down into a place unknown. While standing in a gloomy wet room with musky stale air, 'had you tilt your head to look above,' only to find out that it was pitch black.

The crinkles that were wrinkle upon the walls made one notice where does the age and tears come from? As we gathered our senses, we began to wonder is this a tunnel or cave? "A slight glimmer approached, and it seemed to stare me in the face!" 'I heard a noise that came from behind and as we turned to look there was nothing there,' and when we turned back around "the vision of light was gone!" We questioned this unusual surprise that has 'suddenly opened our eyes.'

After gazing amongst the paths, trying to determine which way we should go, undecided about making a choice, led me to sit down and ponder about it for a while. "A strange sensation crossed my mind," 'maybe this is a daydream and somehow we convinced ourselves we got caught in a nightmare!' I thought how preposterous someone's imagination can stretch when they find their-selves in an unpredictable mess. 'Collecting your thoughts with a grin on your face you realize how ridiculous you have become.'

There was a decision that had to be made, 'which direction should we follow?' Looking up to the left there seemed to be a small indentation notched out that you would have to squeeze by. A quick glance the other way looked clear enough to follow. It was a continual steady course going downward along a slope. 'While walking along you were hoping that you would find a way out of this dark hole.'

"Confronted by the darkness you had suspicions," this viewpoint of the scenery, while walking amongst this rocky terrain, allowed you to recognize a peculiar speculation?

'Somehow it caused a distortion to form within the confines of this place.'

"This entrapped feeling finding its way to ride the winds of darkness was playing on the strings of your emotions."

While staring at the other side of the path you came across a steep trench. As you were looking down you couldn't see how deep it was, 'past the misty smoke that was floating up.' "Watching this rising vapor" it seemed to be stuck while dissipating into the night.

'Glaring across the edge of this trail' a platform was carved out on the corner of a stone. This portion of the wall looked as if there was an image acting a part on a stage. Although it was 'taunting me to come up and see,' we were having a hard time believing this was a vision. "My imagination took over and we simply lost control," seeing a facial expression that seemed to glow on a stage wall.

'While focusing upon this illusion it had you wondering with curiosity,' "Am I just exaggerating an imaginary dream that didn't even happen?" As you got closer to the end of the path, there was this 'smoky haze' coming from the channel that was beneath a narrow bridge you had to cross. This was the only trail you could take to see the stage in the wall.

"We heard creaking and squeaking" from each step we walked while crossing the bridge. "It made sounds as if it were crying and weeping from agony" before we reached the other side. 'Thinking to myself had me dazed,' was this bridge trying to tell me something?

'This blind distraction persuaded me' to go up to the stage and we noticed a crack from a door. There was a 'dim lighted shadow' protruding through which bounced off the surface of a wall.

As you got up to the door it was made of stone. Beside the wall you saw a bone lying on the floor and 'thought' I'll use it to pry this stony door open. It never occurred to you where the bone came from. We budged the door to where it was slightly open, enough to stick our head in to see what's in the room.

"It appeared as a marshy bog jungle," inside the room were old rotted out trees and brush, with decaying moss growing on the walls and ceilings.

'While glancing there was an entrance,' "and upon glaring inside this massive delusional dimension it was like looking through the eye of a skull!" Now my curiosity started turning inside my head wondering 'what's through the eye?'

Finding myself pacing around in circles about this 'strange and bizarre notion kept me asking,' How do we get out of this jumble confusion? We were struggling with what decision to make, we found ourselves tugging at the consequences 'should we enter or not?'

'We kept talking to ourselves, insisting what is right,' it appears there's no other place to go.

Should we go through an 'eye of a skull' and what will we find out after entering into a 'dark window of the unknown?' Would we return to the world that we're adjusted to? "The stillness that surrounded me was chilling;" we didn't see or hear an answer! There was no sign or whisper to tell me if we should stay or go.

The possibility of going through had me on edge; a somewhat doubtful "fear seemed to be covering my face!"

"A voice in my head" kept asking me, what was the other alternative? 'An empty look in my eyes' had me wrapped inside a bubble, and stuck in a black hole, wandering around to my own heart's desire.

'My mind was pressurizing me' to make a choice, told me to go through the 'skull to see what's on the other side of the eye.'

As we went through, there seemed to be a "sparkle that flashed," then it vanished, and we found ourselves blind for a while.

After the entrance through the "eye of no return" we looked back and seen we were inside looking out.

The Lost Stairs

For I seem to have tried to wake up while hanging on the side of the mattress bed, looking at a wall with black stitches covering a stone wall. After glancing at this for a moment or so, I thought maybe I was in the wrong apartment. I started shaking the cobwebs out of my eyes.

While waking up this morning, I looked out the second-floor window. I had some orange juice, a slice of toast with butter and jelly while grabbing some clothes to wear. During this morning view, a sudden shake had me whispering after tasting the sweetness of a custard pie.

As I put my clothes on and had my morning eats, I was on my way downstairs to see the world. I wondered if it would be upside down today, like it usually is, when suddenly I tripped and rolled down the stairs. At the bottom of the stairway, it seemed I had bumped my head. Feeling dizzy, I thought I must have been going too fast.

As I struggled to reach the street, I forgot where I was at! I went back to the stoop and sat down on the steps and started rubbing my head. Didn't realize how bad this could be! As I was holding my head with my hands and my elbows were resting on my knees, I noticed my eyes were getting heavy; it appeared that I wanted to pass out.

But with the noises and buzzing running up and down the street, my mind was talking out of control. I couldn't tell who's who or where the voices were coming from. My mental capacity has been somewhat diminished. Can you see I'm falling in, and I can no longer hide!

I began to drift away, thinking later down the road, I believe I was hallucinating; the crowd around me told me about it. Somebody mentioned, "You said I feel." I'll be running in a fast car on a lost lane trying to find a direction. Someone else told me, far away from a lonely list take me down to the water, for I don't want to know my emptiness, take me down to the water and give me your love and seal it with a kiss. Can I walk through water and not get wet or did I get dried off before I realized it?

Something to that affect! I must have been out of it!

The last person remembered something I was surprised of! That was about the time a woman showed up and saw my agony that I must have been in. I heard her soft voice and wavy hair.

Both of them knew what I said, in my delusional state, she said, he said, "I can touch where it would make you whole. I could bless it where you won't get old. I can make you where you don't look cold. I can make you think that you lost control!"

She looked at me stunned with an unbelievable expression. She asked me, "Are you all right? Because you look like something hit you on the side of your head."

My eyes rolled to glance at her. I was all right, then I dropped my head down toward my lap.

I started to pass out, and she kept asking, "What's your name? Where do you live?" She grabbed my head and looked at the bruise, and she told me, I should get some professional help, and I shouted, "No, don't do that."

Then she shouted to the crowd, asking if anybody knew me; they didn't know anything about me. With a worry look on her face, she hesitated and eventually said, "I don't know what to do, and I can't leave you here by yourself." She saw my eyes were rolling again, starting to close when she began shaking me to wake up, then she asked, "What am I going to do with you!"

I murmured back, "Take me with you."

She kept asking, "What's your name? Who are you? Where do you live?" While shaking my head, I mumbled out, "I don't know. Can't remember. My memory, I don't recall." Eyes were starting to get blurry again.

Then she put her hands on my shoulders and started shaking me, hollering, "Don't you pass out on me!"

She got the idea of looking for my wallet that should have his identification. When she opened it, there was nothing in there but money! Aching with the throbbing sounds of booms in my head, I brought my hands up to cover my ears. She questioned me, "Are you all right?" She had to say this couple of times before I could nod my head; I was okay. She said, "Since you can't remember anything, and you don't want to see a doctor, you're in no shape to go anywhere. I'll take you to my apartment. It's about four blocks down. I think you will need to ride in a cab." And then she said, "By the way, I'm Vera. I need some of your money to pay the driver because you're in no condition to try to walk." She asked me, "Is that all right?"

I replied, "Okay," but was a little confused on my answer. Vera also mentioned something about a drugstore and said, "We'll get some bandages to wrap your head and some painkiller for pain."

Before I nodded my head, I was getting woozy again. I could hear her say, "Now stay awake. Don't pass out on me. I'm going to flag a cab. I'll be back."

A few minutes went by, and Vera had a cab, they both saw I was holding my head using my hands. Vera told the cab driver to help her get me in the backseat of the cab. As we were getting inside the cab, she mentioned to the driver about a drugstore on tenth street. When we got there, Vera asked the driver to keep an eye on me. She'll be right back.

In the meantime, the cab driver was talking to me, but I was kind of unconscious, and he wasn't aware of it. When Vera came back out with a small bag of supplies and saw how I was, she started shaking my shoulders to wake me up. The driver was a little disturbed for a minute. I thought he would try to pull Vera off, but Vera yelled at him and shouted, "We need to keep him from passing out." They finally got me to open my eyes, feeling drowsy. She requested, "Now get me to 1846 Tenth and Pine Street, and hurry!"

When we arrived at her address, she insisted to the driver, "Help me get him inside my apartment."

At first, he was reluctant but said, "Okay."

So they took me upstairs and put me on the couch. She turned to the cab driver and asked how much she owed. He echoed a number I couldn't focus on, and she paid it out of my wallet that she's been carrying for me.

The cab driver had some questions to ask her, but she barked out, "I don't have time for that. Would you mind leaving please?"

He said, "All right, I hope everything works out for you guys. If you run into problems, just call the Cab Company and ask for Danny."

Vera said, "Thanks, I might need to. But for now, I need to help him out."

With a curious look, he said, "Well, it's time for me to leave and see if I can make some more beans."

Vera nodded. "Fine, I wish you luck."

He finally left.

She had the bag on the coffee table and went into the bathroom. When she came back out, she had a couple of small bottles in her hand and a cup of water. Vera told me to sit still. It was my turn, and she started opening the bottles and had one from the drugstore. She had me swallow one by one with a sip of water in between. I don't remember how many it was, either three or four pills, but it was a chore for both of us. Somehow I had trouble swallowing right.

At that moment, I started to lean to the side, thinking it's time to lie down, but she brought me back up with a stern look. She said, "Stay there. I need to look at your head!" Then I told her, "You certainly are a persistent woman." She smirked at me and said, "I need to be."

After that delicate conversation (with a blend of sarcasm), she began looking at my head.

When Vera got a closer look, she commented, "Oh my goodness, you have a gash under that big bruise, and the blood has dried up in your hair!" She said, "It's long enough to think about getting stitches." She got up and said, "I have to go and find some scissors. I'll be right back so don't move."

Vera came back with scissors, a washcloth, and some more water and proceeded to wash the area until the hair was wet. Then she took the scissors and started cutting the hair, removing it slowly. Eventually when the laceration was washed and cleaned, she made the remark, "Now here comes the fun part."

I didn't think anything of it. I just wanted to lie down and sleep.

She took her hand and held my face straight. She brought out this reddish-orange liquid in a bottle, while she soaked the dauber. Vera told me, "Hang on. This is going to sting!"

When she started applying this on my head, I jumped and shouted, "Oh shit, that hurts like hell. What are you trying to do to me?"

She told me, "Oh, chill out. It was necessary, so quit being a cry baby." Then she took another look at the gash and said, "I want to apply some more to make sure it won't get infected."

I told her, "You just want to see me scream again!"

Vera giggled on that comment.

At that time, she put a gauze pad on the cut, wrapped it with roller bandage and taped it down and mumbled to me, "I'm through. I will get you a couple of pillows and a blanket. Now you can go to sleep. Tomorrow, we will need to redress it." She smiled and said, "I hope you have some answers!"

* * * * * *

I woke up startled to find myself lying on a couch in a strange setting. I had this weird dream. I dreamt a woman with green eyes and shades sold me a straight cold player and told me to loosen up and don't cry. She said, "Just do me a favor and say goodbye before anything else comes our way! I'm a fire when you think it's cold!"

I thought to myself, *What does all this mean?* While glancing around the room wondering, *Where am I at?* Seeing a dark open window, I was thinking, *Is this morning or nighttime?* I seemed to be confused, and when I started to get off the couch, there was excruciating pain coming from my head! When I touched it, there was a wrapping around it. I decided to sit back down pondering to myself, *What this is all about?*

When I added that with the room, a click came out of my mouth saying, "There was a woman around. Who was she?" And I wondered, *Is this where I am? And who wrapped my head? And why does it hurt?*

I had questions that I needed answers to. Then in my wildest dream, I found myself in a perplexed situation. I questioned myself as if I was a lawyer in a detective movie, "Where is this woman at? And does she live here? And where is here?"

About that time, a woman came walking in with two grocery bags, gleamed at me with a smile, and said, "I see you made it back to the living," while she proceeded to put the groceries up in the kitchen.

I awkwardly asked, "Who are you?"

She replied back, "I could ask you the same question!"

As I sat there dumbfounded, there wasn't an answer I could give her.

She happened to see the troubled expression I had on my face and somewhat feeling sorry for me said, "I'm Vera. I brought you here and helped patched your head. You have a lacerated bruise, and you've been sleeping in my apartment." Vera was perplexed herself. She implied, "Now who are you? Where do you live? And what happened to you?"

I got to thinking for a minute or two and confusion set in. I told her, "I can't seem to remember!"

Vera's response to my bewildered situation was, "That's what you've been telling me all day!"

I asked her, "What time is it?"

And she told me, "It's eight fifteen in the evening," and then she pointed to a clock on the wall.

"How long have I been here?"

"Let's see, since nine thirty this morning."

"You mean I've been here for over eleven hours?"

She said, "Something like that. Now are you hungry?"

Vera causally asked, "Do you like turkey and cheese sandwiches because that's what I'm making?"

With a chuckled, I asked, "What kind of cheese?"

She said, "Monterey cheese."

I said, "That would be fine."

Then Vera was baffled. "What type of cheese do you think I had?"

I told her, "I couldn't stand American cheese. It makes my stomach twirl."

"Amazing don't you think? You can remember about cheese, but you can't remember your own name! What would you like on your sandwich?"

And I told her. She fixed it and handed me a plate and asked, "Would you like some chips?"

And I said, "Yes, that would be nice. Thanks?"

She noticed I was eating well and asked me, "Do you like it?"

I said, "It taste good."

Vera thought, "I hope so. Since you bought it, I've been using money out of your wallet."

I said, "You have my wallet."

And she said, "Yes, I do."

And I commented, "Can I see it?"

And she flipped it to me. While I was going through it, she told me, "There's nothing in there, except some money. I've already tried that."

I went, "Oh," with a defeated look on my face.

With a puzzled glare on her face, Vera had to ask, "Why wouldn't you want help from the doctors?"

With a somewhat distressed feeling, I told her in my illusive surmise, "People in white suits bring death! I figured I owe you that much in helping me out."

She said, "Thanks on your inside paranoia telepathy. I'm sure you're set up on expanding sensory channels to communicate to the minds that are in concern!"

I asked her, "Are you a doctor a nurse?"

She glanced at me and thought, "I think it's time to get out of the psychiatric counseling center." Then she started giggling. "Earth to stranger, earth to you, can you come out of that ball of wax we call space!"

All kidding aside, Vera looked at me and said, "It seems you have forgotten the past. In fact, you can't even tell me how you got that gash on the side of your head."

I told her, "I'm sorry about the difficult spot that I put you in."

She said, "That's okay. I got to practice on my nursing skills, plus I got to spend some of your money. By the way, it's time for you to take some more pain pills. Do you need them?"

My head was still aching; I asked her, "What are you giving me?"

She brought over a glass of water and said, "Take two of each. See if they help, and I'll see you in the morning. I'm tired it's been a long day."

I said, "Good night." When I took the pills in about an hour, I was nodding off sleeping. When I woke up, there was a strange dream that came with it! This dream came my way and told me, "Was time running away from me or was it getting closer than what I thought it could be!"

I saw stairs walking down into the dark, then I thought time was near. Will it cause any fear? Then it went one step further. It said, "Relax, the venture can be risky, but where will the harm come from, for don't you know that you're out of the storm?"

At this point, I got off the couch and started scratching my head; it began to itch. While walking around the room trying to understand this dream, "contemplating what does it mean," it seems that stairs have something to do with the situation I'm in.

Then a flashback came, for when I went out into the hall, I saw stairs going up and down. It came back to me; I fell down a stairway. That's when Vera came through the room out into the hallway, a little drowsy herself and asked, "What are you doing out here?" She approached me and inquired, "Are you sure you should be walking around? And how does your head feel?"

I got somewhat dizzy, but other than that, I felt fine. She said, "Well, you better come back in, and I'll redo the bandage, and we'll look at that gash."

Excited about what I just remembered, I told her what happened to my head! As she was cleaning and redressing the bandage, she murmured, "I'm sure you'll tell me all about it."

With a disappointed tone in my voice, I said, "You don't seem to be as thrilled as I am!"

Vera calmly said, "But I am, I am. What did you just remembered?"

I told her I fell down some stairway, and I must have hit my head on something hard.

Then she muttered, "That's nice." Then I came back and said, "Nice—nice, what do you mean nice?"

Vera then giggled just kidding, "Don't you know when somebody is pulling your leg, then she released an oh-gee-whiz sigh. Then with a more sincere look on her face, she commented, "Where did this all happen? And do you remember anything else?"

I shook my head and said, "That's it." I told her, "I had this dream that led me to stairs, and when I saw them, I remembered that."

She just got finished rewrapping my head, and while I was thinking, it happen to pop in my head. I asked Vera, "Where did you find me?"

She answered back saying, "Yea, I picked you up at Sixth and Oak where you were sitting under the front porch stoop. Half delirious!" Vera noted to herself, "I guess that's where you'll want to go?"

Baffled I said, "You read my mind. But I need to wake up first. Let's have some coffee and breakfast. I'm famished."

As she was washing her hands and suggested, "How about some bacon and eggs with toast?"

I smiled back and said, "That sounds great."

When we were finished with breakfast, I asked her, "Are you ready? So we took a cab back to Sixth and Oak, and there was an apartment house that stood three-stories high."

Vera pointed out the concrete steps leading up to the front doors and sadly said, "That's where the crowd and I found you."

She replied, "Yea."

"All of us thought you were going somewhat delirious the way you were talking, but that's another story." I looked carefully at the steps and outside building and asked, "Vera, let's go inside."

She said, "We can try, and when we went through the front doors, I stared and stood in front of the last step at the stairway that I fell from."

Curiously looking at it, I turned to Vera and made a remark, "This is it. This is where I fell, and I must have hit my head right here on this last big baluster." When I glared at it closer, I saw some dried-up blood spots, and I showed Vera, and she agreed this must be the place! Then she informed me, "If that's the case, then you fell downstairs. Let's go up a flight."

When we reached the second floor, I noticed a picture of a mountain landscape in the hall, in which I thought looked familiar. I stood there staring at it, and Vera asked, "What are you doing?" I shared my thoughts with her, and she said, "You do recognize this place?"

With mixed emotions, I told her, "I think so." Then I went on further, "There seems to be a room up here I was in."

As we were walking by looking at the doors, I had seen this room number 22.

* * * * * *

I pondered looking at it strangely and said, "I think I live here!"

She replied back and said, "Well, knock on the door."

"I tried no answer. Tried again, still no response."

Vera was eager and said, "Try turning the doorknob and see if it's unlocked!"

So I gently turned the knob and opened the door, and it was as quiet as a church mouse on Sunday. As we walked in, I went to the kitchen and looked out of the window, then to the bedroom and noticed the black stitches covering a stone wall, and I stood there and watched it. It seemed to amaze me that suddenly, I realized what this dark image was! It appeared to be an outline of a gruesome shrill, a cry from another dimension, a stairway that led you to the darkest secrets to this building, hidden behind this wall! I could hear echoes of nervous tension coming out of the wall! I saw a vision of a staircase running to the bottom depths of darkness in where I couldn't see the last step.

Vera came in and showed me a family picture; it was my mom, dad, and little sister, and it clicked together. I told her, "That's my family, and I live here. My name is Joel O'Shea." Being dismayed, I hesitated to tell Vera, 'What I had just heard and seen?"

She thought I must be having some sort of relapse. Stunned, I somewhat questioned it myself. Then she began to dispute me and told me, "What have you seen or hear?"

I instructed to her that those black stitches on the stone wall were outlining and representing a location of an entry way that will lead her to a stairway that has no home!

She said, "Go on, you sound as if you've watched to many horror films or have you been talking to the bogeyman?" Vera was starting to laugh about her own humorous comments. And I thought the way she put it, it does sound kind of ludicrous.

As I turned to go back to the kitchen to the refrigerator to see if I had something cold to drink when Vera whispered, "Come back here, Joel. I hear something."

I glanced at her and thought, *Is she going to try to pull a stunt on me!* I just stood there dumbfounded to see how far she was going to go! Using her hand, she waved to me. "Come back and see."

Standing beside her, she pointed her finger to her ear while looking at the wall. But I didn't hear anything.

We stood there for a few minutes, and I finally told her, "I'm going to the kitchen to get something to drink." She stared at the wall, then decided to follow me, and when I looked at her, I mentioned, "Now who looks ridiculous?" We had this weird feeling when we looked at each other, and it seemed to us something was strange about that wall. I handed her a coke and just stared at the room. Vera started looking out of the second-floor window and said, "What do you make of it?"

I was standing there in disbelief and said, "Someone has covered it up."

Vera asked, "How long have you been living here, Joel?"

I looked at the calendar on the wall and mumbled, "About three months."

"What are you going to do about it, Joel, since you see something strange on the other side of your bedroom wall?" She carried on informing me that she couldn't sleep in that room. I told her. "I've been doing it for three months. What's changed?"

"Well, you didn't know any better than!"

I replied, "Yea, you're right. It does give me the creeps." Then I answered back, "How come it waited three months before I was aware of it?"

She just stared at me and didn't say anything. In despair, I thought, *I have nothing to lose. I'm going to find out what's behind that wall!*

Vera pointed out, "You might open the gates to another world if you saw what you told me earlier."

I gave her a funny look, and we went back into the bedroom and seriously looked at the black stitches on the stone wall. After looking at it closely, there seemed to be an outward impression of a spiral stairway leading around in circles. These stitches appeared to be outlines that were scratched in the pale stone of its background. Glancing at it, I was standing on top of the highest part of the stairway. Viewing it toward the center, there was a hazy gaseous vapor that appeared to be floating in the middle of the stairs.

Vera and I looked and saw something I've never noticed before. Glistening shadows with two eyes peering from the bottom of the stairway. The sadness of those drooping eyes looked as if they were lonely, waiting for someone to come by and visit them.

We stared at each other wondering, *Do you see what I see?* A distraught feeling was formed on my face, and I said to Vera, "How did they get inside that stone wall?" Perplexed about this, I decided to look at both sides of the wall. After gazing, there was a closet on the other side of the bedroom wall. It led to the hallway closet room. It adjoined the wall with the stitches running around in circles. I told Vera, "I'm not for sure where this may lead," but I started taking some clothes out of the closet.

I removed the shelves, and I accidentally slipped my hand onto the back wall, and it disappeared inside the wall. I pulled my hand back quickly, shocked by the threat of losing my hand! I shouted to Vera, "I found something weird. There seems to be an entrance or a portal leading inside this wall!"

I showed Vera where I lost my hand in and whispered to her, "Watch out! I don't know where this may lead to."

She asked me, "Do you have a broom or stick we can use? We need to find out how big the opening is."

I whispered about, "Check the kitchen."

Vera brought back a coat hanger and told him, "This is all I could find."

I shrugged my head and said, "Let me see this." He unfolded the hanger to make it longer and started probing the wall. I asked Vera if she could find a marker, something to write with, and Vera said, "Don't you have one in your apartment?"

And I replied, "I don't know. I don't think so."

So she took her purse and looked inside and found some lipstick. She told me to use this to mark the size of the hole.

As I was punching the wall finding the size of the opening, Vera decided to look at the wall in the bedroom, and what she saw was astonishing. The wall was moving back and forth like it was breathing, and there was a sound she heard as if it was releasing a sigh of relief.

She was so overwhelmed she had to tell somebody. So she shouted to me, "You must come in here and see this!" I dropped everything and came in, but when I got there, the wall stopped breathing. Vera was now baffled. She said, "It stopped. Why?" She tried to explain to me what was happening and what she saw, but I nodded my head and told her I was done marking the hole anyway. I did look at her as if she had lost a screw!

We both glared at the wall then at each other, and everything just seemed to sit still. Nothing was happening. Vera gazed at me and frowned. "What do we do now?"

I implied, "We can check out the opening, and I'm thinking about going inside to see what's in there!"

Vera thought, "Why?"

I insisted, "I'm going to check it out sooner or later."

Vera replied, "Yeah, you're right. Well, how are we going to do this?"

I said, "I'm not for sure. I need to think about it!" When I was probing it, nothing happened to the coat hanger. But she did make a comment. She reminded me that was about the same time she saw the wall was moving, and it appeared that it was breathing. Vera thought, "Let's try that again, and this time, I will probe the wall, and you watch it, Joel."

I thought that's a good idea, besides it can't hurt. So I showed Vera the opening and where it was marked, and she commenced on probing while I was looking at the bedroom wall. Still nothing happened, and I hollered to Vera, "You can quit now. Nothing is moving."

Vera came into the bedroom and looked at the wall with doubts written all over her face!

She said, "There's something spooky about this whole thing."

I agreed. I was getting confused on what I should try next. He said, "It all leads up for me to look inside the opening because now I'm getting curious."

We both went to the opening in the wall, and it was too small for both to get inside the closet room. So when I got on my hands and knees and proceeded to touch the wall, Vera was standing behind me.

Now I requested to Vera, "Get down on your knees and hold my ankles while I stick my head inside the wall." As my head entered the wall, Vera noticed my head had been swallowed up like someone just dislodged my head from my body.

She was terrified to see me without my head, looked as if it's been chopped off by a guillotine. Then she mumbled to me, "What do you see? What do you see?" She said it several times and wasn't getting an answer. Vera was starting to get nervous and worried. She thought about pulling me back in toward her.

Then I brought my head back, and with a shaky expression on my face, I stuttered, "It was cold in there, and the dreary darkness had me shivering. It was so hard to see anything that looked stabled. The foamy mist was floating in windy waves making it even harder to see which way I can go." Then I had this chilling, horrifying look in my eyes. "I feared what it would be like if I got lost in there!"

Vera had to calm me down. I was petrified. I kept murmuring about making it back. I thought I was lost! I finally came back to some form of reality and asked Vera, "How long have I been in there?"

She said, "About five minutes or so, but it was the longest five minutes that I can remember."

I said, "It felt like hours to me!"

My eyes were staring in front of the wall; they were fixated. Looking toward the opening, I began to gibber about an image I saw of a stairway leading down into a foggy haze with two white peering circles, and I heard echoes of sullenness cries. The bellows of distorted moans fed fear into my mind! I was starting to shake just thinking about it. Vera was feeling the tension just from hearing it!

She told me, "Let's get out of here."

And I said, "Wait a minute! I need to think—just think."

Vera shook her head and was wondering, *What is there to think about?*

I confessed to Vera that the moans of cries sounded familiar to me, and I said that I needed to know who it was!

She had a distressful look in her eyes wondering, *What does he mean he needs to know?* Vera gazed at me. "What are you doing? What are you thinking? What's on your mind?"

In a dismal sagacious way, I had to know. The fright had past. The fear was admonished. The nervousness had ceased at least for now, and my adrenaline was over stimulating my senses. Vera was witnessing a different type of me that she hasn't seen before! Vera shook me by my shoulders and told me, "Wake up! This impulse has somehow grabbed you, and now you can't seem to let go!"

I looked at Vera and casually told her, "Everything is all right. Don't lose your mind. It will be just fine. Don't worry. It will be fine. Don't worry."

Vera thought, *This isn't right. Who's calming who down?* Dismayed about how things got turned around, she shouted to me, "How dare you try to turn this around on me when it's you!"

I chuckled with a grin on my face. "Turn what around? I'm not trying to turn anything around. Apparently, you're the one who's going somewhat out into the deep zone, not me!"

She stared at me with a perplexed look and thought somehow we had both changed. Vera with a collective coolness thought, *I'm going to nonchalantly stand still to see what he's going to try next!*

I seemed to be aware of what Vera was thinking and asked, "Is it okay? Are we all right? Let's not have this strange awkwardness get in the way because I agree, there is something unusual about the suspicious vibes we happen to sense from one another."

With a distorted frown on her face as she was sitting in one of the dining room chairs, she announced to me she's leaving. I jumped up excited, begged her not to leave. Vera asked, "Why not? I don't want to be here anymore."

I repeated myself saying, "I can't do this without you."

She requested, "What? What do you mean can't do this? Do what?"

I implied, "I can't do this!"

She asked, "What? What you can't do?"

I said. "I can't do it. I just can't do it."

She implored, "Do what?"

"I need to go in there once again."

Vera nervously renounced my implication saying, "No, you're not going. I won't let you."

I said, "I must—I must, and I need you to help me."

As she was sitting at the dining room table, I was standing at the closet room entrance just staring at the wall in the room. Vera seemed to notice a hunger or maybe it was a somewhat trance on my face just gazing at the wall opening inside that closet room. I turned to Vera and rambled to her in a distorted way, "It's ready for me. It says it's ready for me! It asks, 'Am I ready for it? Am I? Am I? Am I ready!"

Vera scrambled to me and grabbed my arm and said, "Ready for what? What are you talking about, Joel? Have you lost your mind?"

I kept saying, "It's ready! It's ready!"

Vera finally calmed me down enough to ask, "What was that all about? You had scared the living daylights out of me, and you were acting in a very peculiar way."

I responded, "In what way was that? I was just saying what was on my mind. I tried to tell you it needs me to visit it."

Vera asked, "Visit who? Who is it?"

At that moment, I glanced away looking at something else. My attention had somehow taken my mind in a different direction. Now Vera was alarmed, and she felt threaten by my action. She knew she was losing me. I was whispering to the opening in the wall, "I'm coming. Don't you worry. I'm coming." And as he was starting to enter, Vera grabbed me and hollered, "What are you doing? What are you thinking? Get back in here!"

My painful eyes cried. "I need to go. I need to. I just need too!" Agony was written on my face. Cold-chilling agony was forming wrinkles on my forehead. It's shrills were tormenting my very being! Vera was hanging on me, and she started crying with me. She could hear the gruesome screams coming from the darkness in the wall.

I had disappeared into the opening in the wall, and Vera's eyes had seen me going down the "lost stairs and out of sight!" Vera had managed to be on the other side of the wall in the hallway and had somehow bumped her head on the doorjamb and was unconscious.

Vera woke up this morning hanging on the side of a mattress bed and was looking at a wall with "black stitches covering a stone wall." After glancing at this for a moment or so, she thought maybe she was in the wrong apartment.

A Tidal of Livelihood

THEY MAY WONDER what this has to do with the moors, the relation of tides, the rising of movements, or even the wastelands of waters above their normal heights. The swamps, the nourishing flounders of peaty moss encouraging delightful hosts of scaly vipers not wanted. Who has need of these and who would want any part with them? I hear the morgue is a good place for them, or maybe any slimy muddy burial plaque would be a cordial spot to keep their throne at.

A flooding of briskly rain brings sustenance to their friendly abode, causing whirlwinds of swirling current to swallow the excess debris from forming along the shores. There dwelling can be unreliable, moving from one place to the next. Above the developing cliffs where the caves have their entrances, the sharp rocks show the pointy edges of their domain.

Encircling the highest peaks as you were looking along the edges was a ghastly mirage of windiness that left you speechless. While glancing over the steepness of the crags a fear of giddiness took hold. Those rugged rocks glaring back at you as if they were whispering a warning. The effect of the ebb tide has shown its lowest form as the murkiness was left behind. This tide springing inward then outward with its foaming whitecaps of streaming lines protruding within the sands and beaches caused things to form along the shorelines.

This breach of texture enabled the seas to bring different formations of interesting particles to collect along the coastal region. There were substances and items washed ashore that the seas have given up for someone to look upon as witnesses. This was the start of an investigation that was brought forth when a satchel case of mysterious antiquities were straddled on the sands of the shore. As a partaker of the discovery, there were four of us who were challenging the seas on that dreadful day. I can say it is now dreaded, but of the actual day, it was a strike the four of us encountered thinking amongst ourselves that we had all become rich. Little did we know how enticing one may lie or cheat within this tight knitted group that we formed along the years. How deceiving, how contradicting, how conniving, and how tempting…that murder could become a part of our scheme of plans.

These temptations of scrutiny that was enveloped amongst one another in such a short period of time should have sent red flags in the air at the get-go. The forewarning of mistrust when first the satchel was opened should have shown or at least sent signals letting us know something was amassed. Trust was an attribute that Pete had a hard time to acquire, but he was the gallantry one from the bunch with his high spirits that he thought was invincible. Along with Joan who thought everybody was out to get her, she had a portion of paranoia, always keeping a watchful eye on things around her. Then there was Suzanne, the mother figure who entrusted that everyone thought the same way she did, and she would in turn give the people around her the benefit of the doubt, hoping they would give her the same treatment. And at the bottom of the list was Carl, who thought he was smarter than rest of them. What a tangible group of friends that relied upon one another when their journey began to entrust to each other the value of what true friendship would be about.

When this somewhat unexpected case was found along the coastal seashores, it was Suzanne who witnessed it first. A gleaming sunshine happened to spark a glare coming off the beach in which she saw from the remotest part of the shore where she was infatuated with seashells in the sands along the ocean lines. She pointed out to Joan who was standing beside her, and she thought being the start of a new day it was just a reflection coming off the rocks from above. They both didn't realize the impact of a shiny speck and how it would control the rest of the day.

While Pete and Carl were out into the surf enjoying the carefree livelihood of swimming in the seas, wishing they had a surfboard to ride the waves. They were reminiscing about the past. This was a weekend they had come together as formal college friends to spend time relaxing from a stressful week of daily work schedules, chores, and other activities that required their immediate attention. It was a break from their busy lifestyles and habits, a time to enjoy each other's company. This was also a time and a chance of boasting, testing each other's accomplishments and bragging rights. Besides it's been quite a while since they saw each other. This was a setup plan from weeks back for a get-together camping and cookout. They all showed up last night for this weekend's rendezvous.

This happened to be a Saturday morning, the day after the first initial visit amongst each other's company.

And Pete had made a comment to Carl as he was grasping for air, stating, "I'm getting a little tired. I need a break. I think I'll go up to the beach and lie down, stretch out some."

Carl looked at Pete and said, "It sounds as if you had too much beer to drink the night before."

And Pete thought, "Who was counting!" He told him, "They went down to easy, especially after a hard day's work and this long drive to get here." He said, "Yeah, you may say I have a slight hangover."

Then Pete looked at Carl and said, "You were doing pretty well yourself."

And they both made the casual remark of having campfire hot dogs with cold pork and beans, chips, and pickles, laughing at the idea: "It's been a long time since we ate that way."

In the meantime, Joan was talking with Suzanne, and she made an interesting observation about how the guys have been acting as if they were all back in college. She reminded, "Suzanne, it's only been two years since graduation, and those guys still act as if they are still roommates."

Suzanne said, "Well, guys will be guys, what are you going to do about it?"

Joan blurred out, "Nothing, just nothing."

Suzanne laughed and thought, "Well, you're learning. Yeah, let the two idiots figure it out."

Then Joan asked, "Suzanne, did you find any nice seashells?"

And Suzanne brought out her small plastic bucket and reached in and took out two of them and said, "Here, look at these. I thought these were interesting. Now put one up to your ear, and you can hear the swooshing undertones of the sea."

Joan tried one and found it sounded nice as if you were someplace else, even kind of dreamy. While Joan was studying the formation and colors of the seashells, Suzanne made the leisurely but curious comment of still noticing the small shiny glare down the beach. Now the way Suzanne was describing it fascinated Joan into listening with more discernment. In fact, Joan had Suzanne point out, "Exactly where did you see this? And maybe let's take a walk and get a better look at this."

Suzanne glanced at Joan and said, "I'm game for it. Let's go, besides there's really nothing else to do."

As they were proceeding down the beach, Carl happened to glare up at where the girls were and mildly admonished with curiosity to Pete, asking himself out loud, "I wonder where Suzanne and Joan are going."

Pete turned to look and thought, "Well, it's probably some girl thing. We'll just watch them from time to time to see what they're up too."

As they were watching and listening to the seagulls and terns, the surf tides swishing in and out, they noticed the seagull's activity and just sat there in silence. The seagulls and terns with their eloquent but floppy tenacity were flying over the seas and the shorelines looking for breakfast, a delicacy of fresh fish jumping in the rocky surfs, flipping in different directions caused from the rushing turbulence within the tides, sweeping toward the shore and crashing into the rocks that were formed along the cliffs. And as they got their meal or tired from weariness, they would settle on top of the rocks on the sides of the mountainous cliffs, waiting patiently for their next meal, and cackling with one another, for they seem to be visiting their kin. There seemed to be hundreds of them flying about looking and talking amongst theirselves.

While they were making small talk and funny gestures about the ludicrous actions from the seagulls and terns, Carl glanced down the coastal shoreline, and with his eyes squinting, he made a rather distressed response! He mentioned to Pete how small the girl's images were appearing and thought they were a lot further down the beach than what he anticipated they would go! Pete agreed but said, "Hey, there on vacation too. Let them go, besides they're going to do what they want to anyway. Right?"

"Yeah, I guess so. But I'm curious of what they're up to."

Pete asked Carl, "What's for breakfast?"

"Well, we did bring a couple of dozen eggs and a loaf of bread. Sounds like egg sandwiches, you think! Why not, let's get a fire going and get the skillet warm."

* * * * * *

As Suzanne and Joan were walking, they were also talking, asking each other why they came, and Joan hesitated but did admit she came to see Pete and how he was doing. Suzanne looked at Joan and said, "You still have a thing with him, don't you?"

She sheepishly said, "I'm not for sure anymore, but that's one of the reasons why I came, was to find out if I still do or not!"

Then Suzanne admitted she came to see Carl and how he was doing. She started gibbering how hard it was to find the right man, and that most of them are narrow-minded idiots. Then she giggled about how her mother used to quote, a statement, saying, "If a man had a brain, he would be dangerous." They both started laughing on that wise insinuation and giving her credit on how smart she really was.

It was time to take a break from this sandy barren terrain with small rocks sticking out of the dry dune sand. When Suzanne looked at the shiny glare, it began to take on shape. It appeared to be a dark object, and the reflection seemed to be getting smaller than what it was before. She motioned to Joan the display, and she thought it looked bigger than what they thought it would be. While glancing at it, they thought it was only about another hundred or so foot up there.

Approaching the dark-soaked satchel, Joan looked at it startled, and then she glanced at Suzanne, and she turned and had a somewhat bewildered look on her face as she looked around to see if anybody was here to claim it. She mentioned to Joan, "What do you think?" She implied, "Let's try opening it up."

When examining the case, there were two heavy-duty leather straps with a shiny lock buckle on each one attached around the satchel case, and of course, it was locked. Suzanne tried picking it up and found out it was heavier than what it looked. She responded, "Oh my gosh, this thing can hurt your back!"

Joan thought, "Let me try." And when she tried moving it, she agreed, and she cried out, "Oh shit, what do they got in here?"

"Rocks!" Suzanne giggled and said, "You didn't believe me ha!"

"Well, Suzanne, what are we going to do now?"

She said, "I don't know. Let's sit here and think about this like two intellectual women would do when they come across a problem."

Joan thought, "Well, we could go and get the two idiots back there to figure it out."

Suzanne grinned and thought, "We may have to."

A few minutes went by when Suzanne said to Joan help me turn this case around.

While Suzanne was checking the case a little closer and between her and Joan moving around the satchel and turning it upside down and in other different positions, they noticed water and seaweed was clogged and trapped inside the satchel case. They did make the remark that this case was about the size of a fair suitcase or a small duffel bag. As they were emptying the case from water and seaweed, they could feel the case was getting lighter, thinking, "If we keep this going, we might be able to haul it around." It felt as though they took and emptied about twenty pounds of water and debris.

Joan wondered, "How in the hell did this satchel float up on the beach in the first place with that much weight!"

Now they thought, "If we could only find a way to open this case up, we would be home free."

They found themselves this far, so in their mind, there was no way they were going to leave without seeing what's inside the case. Joan piped up to Suzanne and said, "Do you think if we could find some sharp-edged rocks that we could cut those straps. Or maybe take the bigger rocks to break the buckles to unleash them off the connection that they are locked in."

Suzanne thought about it and handled them in her hands. Then she replied, "They are a lot stronger than what you and I think. In other words, we could drop this case off the cliff, and it probably wouldn't budge the straps."

"No! No! We need to be a lot smarter than this satchel. It's hard to tell what kind of stringent tests it must of went through before it was put on the shelve for sale."

"Yeah, maybe you're right, but there's got to be a way we can break through it."

"Oh, I imagine there is but…"

"What…what?"

Suzanne glared at Joan and asked her if she had a hairpin since her hair was tied up in the back.

She hesitated and answered, "Yeah, I have one. Why?"

Suzanne thought, "Well, I've seen these detective/burglary movies about picking locks, and it seems to come down to some form of a pin."

With a smug look on her face, she implied, "Are you serious? Because you sure don't look like a lockpicker!"

Suzanne reminded Joan, "Well, do you have any better idea?"

"Well, no, no, I don't. Here's the pin. Try not to break it."

Suzanne shrugged her head and giggled on that reply.

While struggling with one of the locks, Suzanne mentioned to Joan, "Go get that big rock you were talking about, I have an idea."

Joan came back with a stone, it was two sizes bigger than her hand, and in fact, it took two hands to carry it. As Suzanne had the pin in the lock and turning it gently, she told Joan she could hear a slight click, but the lock seemed to be stuck, and it feels like it can't release the connection. She thought, "Who knows how long it's been in the seas, and it probably is rusty from the water and the environment."

She looked at Joan and informed her, "This is the plan I'm thinking. That is, I'll put the pin in there and turn it until I hear a click. I'll remove my hand thinking it might get stuck in that position. Then you take that rock and smack the latch and lock. Hopefully the shock will dislodge the connection. What do you think?"

"We can give a try, Suzanne!"

It took them three times before the latch broke the connection, and they both glanced at each other thinking they did it. Suzanne loosen the strap and folded it out of the way. Joan said, "Well, put your hand in there. Let's see what's in there."

Suzanne, stunned by her reaction, told her, "I'm not putting my hand in there, at least not yet."

Joan, perplexed, said, "Why not?"

Suzanne stated, "I don't know what's in there, could be snakes or something!" She said, "Let's turn the satchel upside down and shake it, see if anything comes out that way."

While they shook it, two small crabs came out, and they seemed to act mad as if someone was bombarding their home. They were snapping their pinchers together while they were walking sideways down by the seaside. They giggled at the crabs and thought they were pretty cute, a little hostile but cute. And as they were shaking the case, a bundle of money came rolling out with some more seaweed! And Joan quickly grabbed it and mesmerized by what she saw and shouted, "Oh my," and began and tried flipping through it, but it was so soggy and wet she couldn't tell how much there was being stuck together. But she knew one thing, they were one hundred-dollar bills stacked on top of each other, and they were wrapped in a bundle. Suzanne, with a loud voice, told Joan, "Chill out. Let's keep shaking this satchel because there's more of something in there." She told her just leave the money off to the side and let it dry out some.

Before long, they had twenty bundles lying out in the sun, and Suzanne was astonished. She said, "There is still some more in there."

Joan was beyond herself with so much enthusiasm and excitement lying all over the seashore. She made the remark to Suzanne, "We're rich! We're rich!" At this point, Joan was reaching inside the satchel with Suzanne and pulling out more bundles of money, and finally reaching toward the last stage, she pulled out a small cloth bag that had a tight string wrapped around the end of it. She handed it to Suzanne, and she studied it carefully, as curiosity started to put a confounded look on her face. Then Joan pulled out another cloth bag and then still another! When the satchel was emptied, there were about fifty bundles of money and three cloth sacks of whatever in the bag.

Suzanne was fascinated about the suspenseful three cloth bags just lying there on the beach while Joan was still trying to figure out how much money there was. Recuperating from this excitable but challenging adventure, they were both a little spent and thought it would be a good time to take a break. While resting, their vocal cords didn't seem to get tired. They were expressing their dreams of how they're going to spend this delightful money that they have just acquired. Then Suzanne thought and said, "Joan, I don't want to bust your bubble, but what if someone is looking for this money."

Joan thought, "Well, tough, it's not there's now!"

Suzanne just giggled and thought, "We'll see what may happen next because I have a weird feeling about this." Then she realized and said, "I'm going to see what's in those cloth bags!"

While Joan was trying to count money, Suzanne carefully took one of the bags and gently opened the top end where it was tied off, and upon looking in there, she saw a sparkle, a shiny glow, crystal transparent color, and thought diamonds, sparkling diamonds. They were so small that she was afraid to take any of them out of the bag. But they just shined like there was no tomorrow, and the sun's reflection glared off them as if you saw a twinkle from a star. She was stunned, amazingly stunned. She had never seen anything like this before. A half of bag full of diamonds, and she thought how dreamy, just dreamy!

As she tied that bag back up real nice and tight, she thought, "I wonder what's in the next sack." As she carefully untied the next cloth bag, she glanced in and saw these shiny enchanting red-colored stones. Now her mind was whirling in different directions, and as she pondered, she thought delicious red rubies, mm—mm, and she thought they look better than the most delicious red apples you could buy. And her impressionable mind was staring at this red ruby, thinking, "Try one."

It was trying to suggest to itself, I wonder how good they would taste. Before she realized it, she took a stone out to get a better look at it and gave it a kiss. Then Suzanne caught herself and started talking to herself, "What are you doing? Put that back in the bag and tie it off before you do something stupid."

Joan looked at her kind of puzzled and said, "Did you say something?"

Suzanne reassured herself by suggesting, "No, no, I didn't say anything. By the way, Joan, what have you come up with? In other words, how much is there??

Her face lit up, and she suggested, "About five thousand per bundle, and I counted fifty of them so about quarter of a million dollars is here." Then they thought, "No wonder the bag was so heavy."

Suzanne thought, "We hit the jackpot, didn't we?"

And Joan looked at her and said, "You finally woke up. That's what I've been saying all along!" Then she asked Suzanne, "So what's in those cloth bags?"

And Suzanne, with a rather hesitated but fast response, told her, "I still have one more too check. I'll tell you when I'm finished."

Joan peeked at her thinking, *She's being a little mysterious, and that's not like her.*

Suzanne waited until she found Joan busy doing something before, she took the last cloth bag and started untying it. And what she saw was a transparent bright-green stone. It even sparkled in a dull sort of way as if you could see some blue in there and some had a few dark spots on them, but they radiated with this astonishing greenish glare just glistening at you as if its saying hold me, touch me, I'm yours. Suzanne had her eyes stuck on these stones as if they were hypnotizing her to grab them. She was collectively touching them, holding them, just couldn't keep feeling them.

Joan echoed out to her, "How are you doing?"

And she said fine and started tying the cloth bag up and tight thinking to herself, *I've never reacted like this before, I wonder what's happening to me!* Then Joan muttered something about what they were going to do next. Suzanne had a doubtful feeling on what they should do next, so she used Joan as a sounding board and asked her, "What you do think we should do! Joan wasn't stupid, and she seemed to realize that Suzanne had her doubt, and that she wasn't for sure of what to do. So she thought, *I'll distract her and ask, "What did you find in those cloth bags, Suzann?.* Suzanne realizing her charade wasn't going to last long, she told Joan, "There was a bag of diamonds and rubies and emeralds, how much there worth, I have no clue. But I can reassure you, they are very expensive! And we are probably talking a couple of hundred-thousand dollars, maybe more. I don't know!"

Joan's jaw dropped. "You mean another couple of hundred-thousand dollars?"

"Yeah, that's what I'm talking about, maybe now you realize, why I'm not for sure what to do!"

"You mean to tell me there's a half of a mill that came out of that satchel?"

"Yeah, something like that!"

"What are we going to tell Carl and Pete?"

* * * * * *

Suzanne shrugged it off, telling Joan, "Let's not worry about that now. We have another problem."

"What's that?" Joan implied.

"We need to get this satchel cleaned up and put everything back in there, then see if we can drag it all the way back to camp without being spotted. It's either that or hide it?"

Joan looked around with a desperate expression on her face realizing that hilly sand dunes were off to the side and there were no roads leading in to get this far and further up there were more rocky cliffs. There just wasn't any way to get down this far on the beach, unless you walk or have a dune buggy of some sort.

After the painful agony set in, and they had the merchandise back in the satchel that they started dragging the bag behind them, each taking turns and taking plenty of breaks. Between the two of them, they were discussing about Pete and Carl and thought, they could have had them drag it, but their little conniving minds were thinking they were going to hoard all the money themselves. Each one giving excuses of why they should and why they really couldn't trust them. "Oh yes," they had it worked out. They were in control. They had all the answers. Greed was starting to form in, and they wouldn't admit it but greed, and its ugly head was setting in.

They were dreaming and exaggerating about all the wonderful things they were going to buy and own. "It was paradise." It was a make believe castle, and they were going to be "queens and conquerors of their own empire." Masters of their own domain. And after their huffing and puffing, it was time to take another break, and they could see they were getting a little closer to the camp. But they didn't see Carl or Pete yet!

Suzanne acknowledged to Joan, "It's time to put our thinking caps on."

Joan replied, "What do you mean? Is it about hiding the money?"

She said, "It's more than just that. It's also about what we've been doing down the beach and how the day has been faring, all kinds of daily inquiring questions. And we need a game plan, and we need to stick by it, so they don't get suspicious, you know what I mean?"

She glanced at Joan and made an intelligent remark saying, "That's another reason why I didn't what to leave the seashells back there. It can help us with an alibi."

Joan was starting to admire Suzanne and her artful deception and conning ways, and she made the comment to Suzanne, "I'm glad I'm on your side." She just smirked from that satisfying conjecture and thought, *She's on my side. One less to worry about!*

When glaring and looking further up ahead, they decided to go a little further and saw there was a formation of more rocky cliffs. They thought that will be a good place to take another break. And that will be the place where we will plan out where we were going to stash the satchel bag and everything inside it. Suzanne asked Joan, "What do you think? Will this be all right?"

Joan cautiously went through the area foot by foot and then proceeded to gander at the direction of the camp and looked at Suzanne. "Where do you think will be a good place to stash it? Or should we bury it?"

She appeared to appreciate the effort Joan was showing. But Suzanne suggested, "Let's put it behind this big rock tonight, and we'll think of another place for later. But for now, we just need to be ourselves when we face Pete and Carl."

It set well with Joan, and they casually walked back to camp. They were gabbing with one another how famished they were, discussing how it would be nice to have an Italian spaghetti dinner or maybe lasagna.

Suzanne said she would settle for a good pizza, and of course, these women were talking as if they were already in their dreamland.

While approaching the campsite, Pete and Carl greeted them and inquisitively asked, "Where you guys have been? We thought you might of ran out on us," with a distorted grin on their face. Suzanne brought up her yellow bucket and reassured them she's been collecting seashells and Joan's been keeping her company. Then she sternly asked, "What's for lunch around here? We're both starving."

When Suzanne said this, Joan had a smile on her face she couldn't help it. It was as if she was witnessing a master at work, at least that's what she thought. Carl mentioned, "We have eggs and bologna for lunch."

And Suzanne chuckled, "I'm not eating that. What else do we have? And I want it now!"

Even Pete barked out, "Well, we could cook this chicken that we have iced down."

Then Carl blurred out being somewhat baffled, echoed, "We could fry them over some hot coals and have potato salad that's been iced down also. But that will leave us a little low on other provisions, in which is okay. We thought about saving the specialty for tomorrow."

Suzanne blurted, "Let's have it now, who knows what tomorrow will bring."

Carl and Pete stared at each other and wondered, "What came over Suzanne? She's being somewhat demanding." They were beyond themselves. They didn't know what Suzanne would do next. It was like she was the boss, and they had all do what she says.

Even Joan was a little concern and spoke to Suzanne in private and asked her, "What gives?"

Suzanne gave her a hint, "I'm keeping them on their toes and off guard thinking if I do that, they will not have any time to think about anything else."

Now that warrant of action was even surprising to Joan. She thought, *Has Suzanne gone berserk? Has she gone nuts field!* No. On the contrary, she was putting everybody else on the defensive side on purpose. But in her allusive mind, she had to start getting other people suspicious amongst themselves. That was her goal in order to keep herself from being suspicious.

That evening, when they were nourishing on their chicken and potato salad and drinking in a format of prestige glamour, they were all in a fashionable ball consisting of princes and duchess when Joan and Suzanne were most favorable. They were being so delightful and pleasant. It was as if Pete and Carl didn't recognize it. It was because of their fault, no one else's, just theirs, that the women remembered. There rudeness was appalling in their eyes. They could never dream what they found fascinating in them before. There typical posturing and gloating was unbecoming in the eyes of Suzanne and Joan a delinquent joke. They seemed so degenerate and vile they thought who has use for them. There exhilarated hoop and hollering was getting unbearable as their drinking seemed to come to the point of faster the better.

They were enjoying the competition of who could drink faster than the other. This barbaric action was just not suitable within their prestige of honor. They reminded each other, "We are queens now!" They questioned, "What are these buffoons trying to prove within themselves? Is it ignorance in part of their upbringing? Or is it just absolute unfounded dumbasses in play? This was the picture the girls were contemplating in their ritzy mind that they have just acquired. Somehow or another just witnessing this platter of riches has turned their minds around to notice the average strider. They looked upon each other and thought, "What shall we do with these imbeciles we use to call friends!"

They thought, "Let's do away with them while we still have a chance." But Suzanne calmed Joan down and said, "Let's use our wits about, for we need to come up with a plan. Let's think we'll come up with a diversion to set things straight."

Joan looked at Suzanne and responded, "I'm with you all the way."

She reaffirmed Joan, "This is the only way we can keep control of what is ours."

Joan agreed and started thinking in the same format as Suzanne was, admonishing her decisions with strict style forward directiveness. "Oh yeah," she thought, "this is the life. I'm a queen just as Suzanne is." Evidently Joan was picking up more instructions than what Suzanne had realized when she approached her and said, "Let's do away with Carl and Pete before they find out what we have."

Suzanne glazed at her inquisitively and inquired, "What do you have in mind! For you do realize that this has to be done without it coming back to us!"

She seductively suggested, "We get them drunk as a peacock and in bed with our womanly erotic ways and commit our murderous deed, then put them in the ocean at high tide. This way, they will be swooshed out to sea for who knows how long and maybe the creatures of the deepest depths will make a buffet out of them." A dauntless interruption came upon the mind of Suzanne, and she recognized that Joan was just as deceiving as she was.

She informed to Joan, "Do you realized what you're talking about is murder, simple profaned murder, murder in the deepest form?"

She said, "I realize the consequences, but I tell you this. Nobody, but nobody, is going to take away the precious values of my heart away from me, and I mean nobody."

And Suzanne noticed she had blood in her eyes. Suzanne had to quiet her down and agree with her terms just to keep her still for a few minutes while she thought about what just happened! Suzanne didn't imagine this in her wildest dream, but she realized she had gone off in the deep inn, and she's taking Joan with her. It was as if Suzanne had looked in the mirror and found Joan there.

Then in her sick mind, there was no excuses or any form of denials or hatreds or even any stressful tension. It was a matter of justification. Yes, as simple as that, justice. She felt that was what society owed her, simply justice. For she was twice renounced on her scholarship that she felt was justly deserved. In her recoil of her history, it was a torment that she lived, without any surface of its spoils ever coming back. Her denial of attending her first two years ate a big groove in her past. She was one of the few who would holler, "Give me justice or give me death."

Suzanne was now petrified with her own anguish and thoughts wondering, *What should I do now? I'm questioning my motives, my objectives, my own heart's desires. What are they but dust in the wind?* And Joan was sitting beside her listening to her confession. She kept apologizing to Joan saying over and over, again and again, "I'm so sorry. I'm sorry. I didn't mean to let it go this far, really I didn't."

When Suzanne started crying, Joan joined in and started crying, and they both hugged each other as if they were inseparable from each other. They eventually realized they brought out the worst in themselves, but they also noticed they brought out the best in themselves.

When it came to Pete and Carl, they just stayed as distant friends, and there wasn't much association with them anymore. But ironically Suzanne and Joan found they were calling or talking with one another on just about a daily basis.

About the money, it was reported stolen, and the FBI and Police departments with the help of certain mob members identified where they would probably find it.

Of course, they had the supervision and assistance of two anonymous citizens.

A Dark Window

A SUSPICIOUS OPENING was observed while it was forming between the panes of an object, "conjuring a tension of unseen suspense!" Amongst the unsuspected sashes of wood, you look upon a substance that becomes a fright. Do you recognize the blankness that forms within a frame?

This quietness that looms outside the casement has a way to open your imagination, trying to guess, "What have I just seen?"

Witnessing an appearance that showed a reflection as it floated by the shade becomes a delirious reaction of terror! Would the mind disrupt itself, not understanding the awareness it started? Could it somehow settle its own illusions? This blindness of one's eye, has it led you to overreact and put your intense fear into shock? With blackness of darkness overwhelming your thoughts and causing your conscious to see unseen shadows that aren't even there, you find yourselves hiding your eyes behind your hands.

Looking upon this delusional bleakness, there is an agitation occurring that seems to keep you surrounded in this "inconspicuous glass!" A prominent foregoing of one's own belief has been shattered!

"The windows of torture pursue against the glass" and the "darkness remains!"

When the storms of extremity pound the surface of the mind, a discourse of calamity and virtual drama has affected your thoughts. An appearance of shadows reflects through the glass while they're dancing from the light of the storm. When you see this, frightful fear has put you beyond the realization of reality! Your conscious keeps wondering, "Will I ever see the other side of darkness?"

Focusing along the edges of glass, you ask, "Is it transparent? Will it help me control the visions of darkness that seems to have a hold on my thoughts?" Or maybe the desire of the unknown darkness is curious and draws you within your soul! You ask yourselves, "What is this to become?"

As you look into the window of darkness, an unforeseen image glared back at you, and what you saw was a shadow that looked like you, "smiling," traced in white outlining!

Your face turned as white as snow when this impression of you was "laughing at you."

* * * * *

This dreadful window glass with its sneer so ever near "was taunting me" and jokingly playing on my frightful fears of darkness that's been haunting me in a room inside my head. I tried to turn away, but this crackling sound like thunder shook the house I was standing in. A thrust of light tossed me on the floor as it projected itself through the dark window and captured a "reflection of my soul."

"My mind was stumbling" as I was crawling trying to get away! When I looked up toward the "dark window," it just stood on the wall glancing at me. While I got back to my feet, "curiosity had me looking around the room I was in." The condition of the room didn't seem to change but then an unpredictable climax showed up with a picture forming on the wall. This window brought forth images of the unknown. In the realm of your composure, the window promoted a conflict with a frightening impression that the glass has shattered!

How did this "dark window" enter into the thoughts of my mind? And "as we looked at the window closely, the glass was still there!"

A chilling sensation overcame me as I looked at the window, and I saw the dew was running down the glass! This dark deception of water striking the glass in small droplets had me shivering "as I watched it" bouncing and pinging off the floor with a stillness of thumps.

This silent dripping splash would fall as if it was in slow motion hearing slight muddling sounds of blobs! As soon as we looked away, the rain, the water, and the drips were gone!

"Now I knew my mind was going delusional." I'm seeing things that aren't there!

"Then I heard the darkness laughing," the window was smiling, and they both had me shaking with terrifying looks on my face. Then that was when the winds came howling, beating its drums with the "window of pain."

The glass, with its big panes, was showing images of the wind while it was whistling a tune of doom! I tried to leave the room, but the doors were locked. "I was on the verge of screaming!" I found my tongue was all dried up, and I couldn't utter a sound. I saw myself sitting on the floor with my hands covering my face wondering, "How am I going to get out of this house?"

Quietness surrounded the room I was in. As I looked up from where I was sitting, the window with its dark glass just stood still on the wall.

As I stood up with my back to the window, I heard a voice from behind saying, "I want to get another glimpse of your fear!" A distraught feeling came rushing to my eyes, and I suddenly turned around to look at the glass window in its frame. With tears of sadness flowing from the dark glass, the window ledge was holding back its terror. The "face of its lips were talking in riddles," murmuring, "Have you had enough fright from me this day? Will the darkness continue with the shadow of its blackness? Have you seen the window with all its different shades? Will there be murder from the glass in the frame?"

"The dark window just stared at me." The glass had some light reflecting itself toward a hollow wall. A frightening image appeared as the "dark glass" began to bleed through the sashes of its panes! The blood was running along the glass as it was spilling down upon the inner ledge. The "window was crying, shouting out in pain!" The darkness with its laughter was amused as the panes of the window were weeping.

Confusion set into my mind, watching the window being tormented by the darkness that hides in the shadows. What I saw from the window had me in fear, and then with a sudden flash, a ghostlike appearance flew from the dark window. His hands were reaching out for my throat, and I jumped back to get away, and the ghostly mist went back into the window.

"Then the darkness of the window just laughed."

This eerie feeling with my neck so close to a ghostly noose had my face in shock, and a "cold-chilling look was in my eyes!" I thought, *Will this ever end? Or have we entered the gates of the unsuspected black coal of darkness? Will this encircle the very core of my mind?* The dark window looked at me with a grimly smile and answered my thoughts. It brought forth a skeleton holding its skull in his hands! His steel-cold eyes were shining red, and the mouth opened with rotted teeth and said, "Come with us, and we'll show you the way!"

My thoughts and vision were vivid, for I could see traces of hair and even cracks in the skulls head!

The darkness of the glass invited me to "come see for yourselves this enchanting dimension that lies within." Its exquisite voice said, "Come, visit us. All you need to do is 'walk through the gates of the dark window,' and you'll be with us forever."

The way his smooth hypnotic words were coming from the glass it started to put me in a state of sleepy illusions. As I was stepping forward toward the window of glass, the darkness was trying to coax me into coming faster. When I came within three steps from the wall where the window was sitting, the darkness brought his arm out of the glass and said, "Here I'll give you a hand!" As I was beginning to reach out my hand, my mind happened to wake up from the reflective glare of the glass, and the tone of his voice had shaken me up. With a sudden response, his hand tried to grab my arm, and I quickly moved back.

The glass in the window echoed out, "You almost made it. What happened? Are you afraid of us? We're here to help you so you may join us and see the dreams that we see." His eloquent voice was shrewd, thinking I would fall for that again.

I stood across the room and shouted to the dark glass, "What do you want with us?" And there was silence in the room, and the "dark window" just hanged on the wall. Sitting on the floor in this empty room, I pondered from weariness in my frightening bones, and the blurriness in my bloodshot eyes had me fixated on the dark window. The steamy perspiration from my forehead was slowly dripping down into my eyes as I was continually wiping the sweat off my face. "This window with its dark glass" had me literally shaken in my shoes, and my skin had become clammy, just looking at its frame and ledge.

It appears the darkness saw the condition I was in and started haunting me with images of ravens flying in the glass. The shadows of wings fluttering with loud swooshing sounds as I saw the tips penetrating through the dark glass. Then the lustrous shiny beaks of these large black birds were peeking around the sashes of these panes as they were trying to make themselves visible before attempting to enter this room I was in.

Trapped in the farthest corner of the house that I could find without taken my eyes off the window, "I heard the darkness laughing," and "the glass reminded me it was not to late yet!"

Watching these ravens pecking on the glass, trying to crack an opening so they may break through, had me petrified into thinking, *If they do get through, what will they do to me?* I saw the heads of these voracious hostile beaks protruding the glass, "screaming with loud shrieks and laughing with their harsh cackles toward me!"

Their wings were flapping so hard and steady against the dark glass, you could tell they wanted out "badly!"

I could hear in the background the "laughter of the darkness" while the glass was echoing the words, "I told you so…I told you so," and he kept repeating those words "over and over again and again!"

My mind was spinning with delirium as these ravens kept screeching with piercing noises that struck the very core of your nerves. Even the marrows in my bones were aching with excruciating pain. This intense feeling of numbness was scorching my feet while I stood there in shock! All of this was happening as the "darkness kept laughing," and the "glass of the window was smiling." The dark window opened its frame and said, "Won't you come in!"

From exhaustion, I fell to the floor. My eyes were closed, and when I came to, there we were lying down all crunched up on the floor. There was silence in the room, and the dark window just stood still hanging on the wall. Now my senses came back and asked me, "Where did the ravens go?"

Thinking about this for a few minutes while everything seems to be quiet, I couldn't quite remember what happened next. My mind has somehow lost itself in a place that I don't know.

I stared at the dark window as it just stayed still, not making a peep or sound. In fact, it was so quiet I could hear myself breathing. When I moved so slightly nudging my way a couple of inches at a time, I could feel my foot breath! I thought to myself, *What is the window thinking?*

"I could hear my heart beating against my flesh," and it beat faster and faster, and now I feel my heart throbbing and throbbing so fast that I thought it would jump out of my chest! I was so terrified that the window would hear me that I was grasping for air! I was holding my chest in with both hands and hoping the window wouldn't hear my heart thumping as I do!

Slowly moving inch by inch going toward the door, and when I reached it, I tried to turn the doorknob, and we were still locked in this room of horror. When I looked back at the "dark window," it glanced at me with a smile on its glass! My eyes, my heart, and my very soul just shut down in weary isolation, staring at the floor, ready to just let my mind go delirious in a deep unknown form of insanity! As my mind was running around in a dark room, it was seeing images of different colors turning small circles in front of my eyes.

I thought, *Oh no, am I going to pass out again?*

Fighting within myself, I fell next to the door, rubbing my face and head, trying to keep myself from going mad! I could feel the fear crawling on my skin; I was scratching my arms and legs and shouting, "Get off, get off me, get off me!"

The darkness started laughing, and the glass just smiled!

I glared back at the dark window and said, "Shut up, just shut up, I don't want to hear you. You're not going to make me go crazy. No, you're not, no, you're not. I won't let you. I won't let you!"

While the darkness was laughing, the dark glass chimed in and said, "Come on in, come on home, we're ready for you!"

Suddenly I heard a faint voice crying out, "Let me out, let me out!" The darkness of the glass whispered to me, "Do you know there is someone hidden in the planks of the floor? He's been mutilated and cut up in little pieces, but he still talks from time to time. Can you hear his heart pulsating as I do? Can you hear his breathing ever so slightly as I do? Do you know he's waiting for you? He's crying out to you, 'Help me, help me!'"

The darkness of the window was laughing while the glass stood still! The silence of the room was so still; I began to think I could hear somebody under the planks of the floor. This feeling of someone underneath me led me into a frightful fear! Why would he be calling out for me? The eerie thought about this dreadful horror was, "is it real?" A nervous anxiety dwelled inside me as I heard it again; it was saying, "Please, please let me out!"

Now the tension of my nervousness increased as I heard the sounds of breathing coming through the slats on the floor. The agony of looking at the floor then at the dark window, trying to keep my eyes on both things, was getting intense. I was struggling with my vision to keep it intact. But the murmuring voices I heard through the floor had me anxiously thinking, "What's below?"

Then the calmness of the room was silent; a weak frail sound of a thump was echoing into the air. The thump was getting "loud and louder and even louder" in my ears. It was as if a heart was beating inside my head! The pressure expanding into my mind seemed trapped! Being crouched over, I could barely keep my focus on the floor, and when I looked up, the glass in the window was smiling once again!

I thought if I had a pry bar, I'd pull the planks off the floor and kill that throbbing sound that continuously pierces through the soul of my mind!

The noises seemed to be quivering their harsh exertion through the passages of my eardrums. The madness of this continuing strain was building up so slowly within; I had my hands over my ears, and my eyes were rolling under my closed eyelids trying to get away from this excruciating fear!

Then something suddenly happened; I collapsed on the floor with my head between my knees and hands still covering my ears. I must have passed out!

When I woke up in a cold sweat, I wiped my forehead and found blood on my hands. I dried my hands on my pants and cleaned my face again and found more wet blood! I looked at this in shock. Where's the blood coming from? Feeling my temple and forehead, small rising gashes were spilling blood from my face! Busted veins were protruding through the flesh, and my nerves were so shot that I thought I'm going mad, stark raving mad. The madness" has caught up with me!

In a prostate position, "I was laughing about in madness." "I had lost my sanity." I got up off the floor and looked at the dark window, and I ran right through the window, and that's the last thing I remember.

They say I was found the next day. Couldn't understand why he would go through the window? And I thought Norman was a leveled-headed man! If he wanted to go outside, why didn't he use the door? There are so many questions of why he did what he did. The police detectives came up to the conclusion that this was a case of suicide. The neighbors were beside themselves when they heard the final outcome.

Beyond the Bones

ALONG A CREVICE canyon, walking the border's edges, glancing down in a darkness of the unknown, there were sounds of a cry, bellowing voices as if in agony, echoing against the hollows of walls.

Screech's dancing from the halls of caverns initiated a gathering destined to fulfill the horrors that came out to play! Who can quench this unavoidable condition as the hollering shrills keep annoying the trees that try to live along the mountainside?

The echo of the forest was whispering amongst theirselves, deciding if it would be all right to let loose the emotions they have stacked up.

Chilling screams would come out to announce their whereabouts, allowing the fright to send high-pitched sounds to those who are within hearing sight!

What would it take to swallow up the "ghosts coming from the bones" that have been lying on the ground?

As the "bones rested on the floors" of the charnel, there was a rattling commotion, sending reflections of sounds bouncing off the surfaces of stones. These shrieking noises would repeat theirselves ever so often! They seemed to enjoy the awakening of life that was circling within so nobody would forget them. Searching farther into the past life seemed to etch a glitch that tried to slide away from reality.

We seemed to be lost inside this misery that shows no mercy while looking for the way out. Will this be an inevitable destination awaiting us at the end?

A glimpse from a passing shadow has given you a view, and while it fleeted away, it happened to brush against you! This piercing contact astounded you and brought us back to a room that was unforeseen.

"An illusion seen in a prison cell" was constantly calling out, asking me to open up the cage, and that he did nothing wrong. They were holding me against my will, allowing me to be tormented day and night! Could you let me out to set me free?

"Bewilder I was for there was only a wooden shepherd's staff" holding him to be!

This traveler, when let loose, walked so fast. The pace was getting faster and faster enough to change appearances and alter the attire of its form while crossing behind the interior barriers of columns, looking for the door!

Trying to bring some sense to this delusional fright had me asking, "Where are we at? Who is this lonely soul that keeps saying to himself, 'Where did this come from? Have I done something wrong?'"

This fear was introducing itself saying again and again. "Once schooled, allows another one to be fooled. Once schooled, allows one to be fooled!" Repeating these words "over and over" had you wanting to get away!

Will the dreadful blackness that surrounds the exit extinguish the emptiness that seems to have you sealed, wondering to yourselves, 'Is there a place to go so I can get away?'"

Standing inside this dust-covered cavern with a stunned look on your face as you kept staring at the rocky ceiling, you question yourself about the situation that you fell in. While glancing around, trying to find a way to get out, doubts start pounding inside your head!

Confusion has set in to lead you to an unbelievable dream. You find yourselves sitting in the dust with your hands holding your head up, while your mind kept spinning in different directions.

This oblivious trance has sent your imagination on a trip while you're looking for the lost forgotten path. You keep asking, "Is this real?" You find yourself trapped when this "foggy smoke starts appearing."

A circling of "ghostly shadows" came in from different places to attend! A surprised ritual formation was beginning. A vision of these hazy mists were floating along in the air. This appeared to be a gathering; while we were watching them from the corner of our eye hiding ourselves behind a wall. Complete silence was staring at us in the face! A terrifying threat was haunting us as they were looking for the bones in the cave. My thoughts as I looked around, "Was I sitting in the charnel of the in carnal host?"

Their devotion was to "bring life to the bones;" raising the bones up to bring them together to create a form that allows the bones to hang in the air! All along, rattling these bones in their hands, thinking during this ceremonial worship this would help wake up the dead!

During the assembly, one of them announced to the others, "It's time to begin the ceremony for the bones to come back to life."

And their religious practice started with an opening shrill that sent chills through the cave. Then suddenly you heard a cold voice chanting, and behold a "rattling of bones" was moving about in the dust!

As the winds blew through the openings of the cave, we saw the bones come together, "bone to its bone!"

And as they were standing upright, I heard a troubling voice saying, "There still is no flesh or breath of life in them!"

Still another said, "Give it a chance. We need to keep chanting so we don't break the spell."

As the bones hung in midair, there was no change. Everything they've done has stayed the same. They asked amongst themselves, "Who has the wisdom and power to overcome this dilemma? How do we put flesh on these bones? And who can breathe life into them?"

There was a grumbling noise amongst theirselves. There was no magical incantation or any other means to bring life back to these bones that they knew of. Their uttering shrills of disappointment, you could hear it pass the opening of the cave. This was what's causing the fear on the mountainside. The "horror of witnessing" this act had me in a nervous fright! This had us shaken from fear; we had to cover our ears from this intense high-pitched tone. Sounds were bellowing and echoing against the eardrum.

Even the hillside was willowing in agony from the torment of shrills running down the mountainside! The terror the trees and grass were facing caused them to hover, trying to get away from the shivering cry!

When the ceremony had ended, the bones fell back in the dust, and the ghostly images have left. When we saw the bones on the dusty floor lying there still, we picked one up and noticed the hardness of these bones. Some were all dried up causing them to become brittle, and when they fell, some had cracked.

We thought, "Will these bones ever wake up to live? When will we be delivered from a hollering shrill that keeps waking us up?" Our cries were not heard following the anguish voices coming from others.

One may shout and try to disrupt the cage that you were left in. But as time goes by, you start to focus on the events that got you there.

Will they ever let me out of this cage that I'm stuck in? Or will I have to listen to the "madness of shrills" for life locked in a prison cell?

Glowing Ghost on the Road

On the side of a riverbank, veering off up a steep hill in the middle of its darkness, "I heard a trampling noise," glooming in the shadows, silver horses running by like ghosts in the night. This sudden galloping thump sent shrills flashing by as the vision took you by surprise! A trembling feeling was sensed watching these "wild horses whining and sneering while glowing in the dark!"

It looked as though they were running toward a goal they were seeking for. Within moments, they were across the next hill, and it became dark once again. I was petrified thinking, "Where did they come from and where are they going?"

While they ventured out of sight, I started walking again, and before long, we were noticing water in the river was "gleaming brightly." It shined enough to bring us light.

And as we were quietly turning in circles, curiosity struck my face as I question myself, wondering, "Where this is coming from?" Within a couple of seconds, we saw a flash coming down the river toward us!

As the gleaming blindness had ajar us, looking at a dreadful sight, the screaming sharpness took the image and sent it forthright going up the river before it disappeared around the bend. While this whirling light came next to me, I found myself lying on the ground beside the riverbank, trying to hide from this spinning glow.

I began to rub the debris from my eyes as we were looking at the river, hoping the allusive light had disappeared. We began to hesitate, asking ourselves if it's safe to get up. While lying on the ground, we were focusing on our bearings, debating on which way should we go.

After collecting my thoughts, we started proceeding up the river again. "About this time, a howling wind was approaching with its intense cool breeze that knocked me off my feet." My instinct told me to lie in the ditch that was beside me, hoping I would escape the brutal torture, in which it looked as if it was coming my way.

The winds were blowing so hard that the trees were leaning halfway down toward the ground. They were giving out weird signals of creaking sounds you hear from rusty old hinges.

This crackling noise was chilling to hear, constantly gazing at the trees that were threaten, wondering if they could hold up under siege the winds were forcing.

"I heard wild voices" flowing along this bottom wetland with glowing lights crossing the hills and meadows showing a dominance that could take things away.

I kept my head on the floor inside this dirt ditch until the fright went along, following its own course. When the blistering wind went over the hills, I decided to sit still and wait. Now after this affect had gone on its own twirling trip, things seemed to calm down a bit, so we proceeded to glance around to see if it was all right to stand up.

This bewilderment had my mind finding itself in a self-hypnotic state, "dazed," asking myself, "Is it okay?"

After relaxing and trying to catch my breath, it appeared my sanity had run across a delusional experience that was unexplainable.

Well, eventually we got back up on our feet. We found ourselves wobbling some before we commenced going to a direction I thought we knew.

Mind you, I'm still out here at night, where the forms of life seemed to be as black as if my eyes were closed with no rays of light. The only thing that was transparent was my hands if I stuck them in front of my face. A somberness swept my mind feeling as if I was a lost child in despair locked in a dark attic.

As I was traveling further down this supposedly lonely road, we saw a formation of "glowing coming toward us" from a distance. There seemed to be a long glow coming down a slope on a trail they were taken. While watching closer, there seemed to be a big crowd straddling and choking the path they were on, coming along toward my direction.

This vision caused concern. Confusion wrinkled my face. Should I hide or run to another place not known? They seemed to be marching in stride with one another as if they had done this before. It appeared the closer they came, the "glow of their shiny brightness" seemed to project an unbelievable sight "like a ghost coming out of a tomb" or were they dancing their way out of a gloom?

Peering behind a tree, I noticed their appearance. They were frightfully hazy while they were walking pass me. "Their faces were glowing" as they were wearing sparkling white robes that were dragging behind them.

"This vision had completely stunned me;" "they reminded me as ghostly priests going off to mass!"

My imagination inspired me. This was there time to set themselves free for a little while before returning back to the crypt from where they had come from. While I was peeking out from behind the tree, I couldn't see how many were traveling on this path of darkness.

I guess they didn't see me or maybe they didn't care while I was watching them walking by me.

As they were walking, I heard them talking in a language we didn't seem to understand. "Thinking to myself they had me intrigued," and my curiosity put me in suspense, wondering, "Who they are?" Not knowing what to do next when the last of them went by put me into an unusual spot. "As part of me was terrified," watching someone from the unknown, but another part wanted to follow them.

I made a decision to back track and follow them from a distance. This move got the better of me. My curiosity took me by surprise, wondering to myself, "Where are they going? I had to know."

While walking along this dirt road at their usual pace, they seemed to look at each other with voices unknown, signaling to each place they've been, where they are going, and what to do upon arrival. I was amazed they didn't seem to realize I was around watching their moves.

Not taking any chances, we decided to fall back a little further, for I didn't want to get caught. I wouldn't know what they might do.

But the next thing I knew, we came upon a sharp curve and blocking the view to the path were thick trees and humongous rock boulders, and this long glow of ghosts were around the corner by the time I got there. And when I arrived, they had all disappeared!

"Astonished" I found myself talking in the cold air asking, "Was this a delusion?" There was something I did notice while gazing around. The sun was beginning to rise, peeking through the hills and trees. Would this be the reason they had all vanished because of the sunlight?

Deception with a Laughter

SOUND OF MERRIMENT is being enjoyed by pleasuring the craftsmanship that's been skillfully laid out for dishonest intentions. Some may get a thrill from fancying their clever cunningness to get away with something, even disputing from doing anything wrong.

Expression of amusement may play along, receiving an achievement that wasn't deserving. Has someone deprived another from receiving a settlement that was due to them?

The giggles and smiles of smugness contended with the accomplishments that one has stole.

Arrangements of one's affairs have been cleverly expedient, using the authority for their advantage while twisting the facts. One may pronounce a seizure of legality and be advised if they went through these steps, it would be granted.

Along the strategy, actions were explained to believe oneself in an advantageous position. The artful trickery of this mindful ingenuity has inflected the divisiveness that was executed prior to the actual engagement.

There has been a lot of discredit trying to summarize the disposition of the illusion.

In the innovation of resourcefulness, you may give the needs to allocate the premise and set up a time to initiate a parley.

As your thoughts come and go like a tumbleweed blowing in the dust, finding the inquisition that's been written for a debate, could cause negative reactions. The boldness of getting somewhat con from an opposition should boil someone's blood.

Hopefully they may have the discipline to be tactful with a plan of action that may disable and burn out the spark of their swiftness.

Will the questioning of another's tampering (caught in the act) disavow any knowledge in which led the questioning in hand? "Can a variance of truth cause a discrepancy?"

There have been situations whereas a persuasion of truth was made on a statement and offered certainty of evidence, but the judgment was ruled invalid, and the circumstance was evaded again! Has the laughter from coercion been involved in the ruling?

Has the deviation of standard agreement been broken within the conflicts, deceiving another victim, and you see the ridicules start pouring in?

Of course, the truth is still out there ready to be discovered.

Do not mind the so-called ability of another's confidence of distraction.

A repudiated refusal to accept or submit and calculate a plan to deceive a fact that's been proven could be detrimental in a case of fraud or collusion.

This delusion may come down to expand a pressure beyond the breaking point, whereas the individual involved that initiated the coercion may have to explain in deep detail, do you know anything about this so-called deception?

"Where would their laughter be at now?"

Hilarious and funny accusations that have people shouting back and forth inside a tormented confine disclosure allows someone to eradicate their temperamental manners! This posture of excitement has one forgetting their natural behavior.

You hear probabilities on both sides of the equation, and you will not find any remorse but maybe laughter! "Jokily evaluating how ridiculous the other one's statement is!" Cruel and profound words start echoing out of their mouths. The whole affair needs better judgment to evaluate the circumstance.

A match between opponents that has a measure of authority and control supersedes the minor display that may even have the truth! Should this have been known at the beginning? Or have we been deceived with dishonoring laughter!

Can we mirth in the gaiety of joyful delight and run with the flow of contentment? Or does the practice of petty division split us to a demoralized invitation to keep going in the same style and unsustainable pattern that compromises the truth?

The buffoon who recognizes a bleakness of sorrow has tear drops painted below the eyes to express the endearment and the sadness of laughter is still within the soul.

Has gladness allow hope to encourage a sneak preview of what you're going to go through.

"Sometimes when you find out, it's too late!"

Rock Stone Bridge

WITH PATCHES ATTACHED to the legs and arms, a rambling shade of blue was walking and talking, having no idea of what to do. It straggled alone off the trail, roaming in a despondent hopeless manner. A mesmerizing temptation was walking alongside, glimpsing at different forms of objects.

They were captivating her divine attention to where she couldn't seem to let go. I noticed there was an unusual problem circling around this woman. It looked as though her mind was tripping with a shadowy face of gloominess and silence portrayed a state of dispersion!

I asked if everything was all right; she didn't respond with an answer. So I asked again and still no change. I question her saying, "Do you see something that doesn't belong here?" But it didn't seem to faze her. I was getting nowhere.

She appeared to be in a deep inner vision of an image beyond my speculation! I found myself sitting on the sand wondering about this situation, *Was I looking through her eyes of dreams?*

Suddenly I heard a voice, crying he couldn't reach out far enough to touch the sky! I asked myself, *Where did the voice come from?* An odd stranger came on the scene; he wore a white beard on his face and was wearing a long red robe and had a hood over his head.

At this time, the girl came out of her delusion, and the visitor said to her, "Are you the one who brought me out and rescued me from my cry?"

She answered back and said, "I believe so. Why do you ask?"

"Well," he thought, "I was curious. Would you help me out if I helped you out?"

She asked, "How?"

The stranger said, "By answering any question you may have will give me a free passage back home. It will give you the answer you may have dreamed of!"

I pondered about his suggestion, and I looked at her and said, "Do you trust this?"

She looked at me then at him and replied, "If you both get what you want and are honest about it, then why not?"

With a suspicious look on my face, I asked him, "First, what is your name?"

He smiled and said, "I'm just a visitor that came by to say hi." As the stranger glanced at us, he politely asked, "What are your names?"

"I'm Jules."

And she said, "My name is Ada."

He acknowledged the introduction and requested, "What will be your answer to my dilemma?"

When both Jules and Ada came up with their question and asked the stranger for the meaning, he came up to sprinkle some hope to the question that nobody knew, and as soon as it was answered, the visitor had vanished!

We had forgotten what we inquired after he was gone! I asked her, "Do you know what that was all about?"

She said, "I think we just left through an opening as if it was a door allowing visitors to enter whenever they wish to. For they seem to come on a path trying to find their way back."

There were times they would get caught and keep them in the cover of the grounds and us in a place that's been iced down. As I was earlier! Jules did think Ada was in another world or was it another dimension?

With his eyesight going fuzzy, Jules didn't seem to notice the disappearance that was happening while he was staring in front of it! The place they were at something has changed. He said, "Oh, I feel something grabbing the heels of my feet from behind trying to drag me back and slow me down!"

Ada thought, "I think we just went beyond this time zone and entered to the next dimension!

Jules stood there watching; she was walking by herself during the night. A dancing light was humming along gathering the harvest of a new song. Jules pondered in dismay. He asked Ada, "Are we going through a dream?"

She replied, "I'm not for sure feels like we are!"

A twinging sensation was following her as if he was a little school boy with a crush. She just looked back and smile. The pleasant gesture in front of his eyes had them bulge out in speechless excitement.

As she was gliding on the road like a butterfly, he started losing sight of her loveliness with the speed she was traveling. He quickly could not keep up and saw she was gone in this misty darkness, a place that had no door!

As Ada said to Jules, "What part of this secluded land are we looking at? These images seem to come and go like shadows playing in the light of the moon." While glancing around, we noticed both have disappeared. "Why did they leave us? And where did they go?" Will we ever know what the condition was, for it happened to fast?

Ada asked, "Do you have any idea where do we go from here?"

Jules, while scratching his head, commenced to saying, "There is a pause in my direction. Let's look at our selection and hope our sense of suggestion would not get in the way of his perfection. It may come to a point where we could go around again and might need to make a correction.

Ada was flabbergasted by my response. She just glared at me with a funny look on her face and pondered, *Are you talking in riddles or using your modern-day philosophy again?*

While walking, we came across and was glancing at the cross on the path and having to choose what looked as if we were in a four-way draw. Ada asked, "Which way, Jules?"

Undecided, he thought, "I'll sit here in the middle of a sand barren intersection wondering to ourselves how we can solve this mystery! When all sides look the same and how long will this moment last?" Ada didn't say anything she sat on the other side looking and waiting.

After a period went by, Ada walked over to Jules and said, you have sat there on the road for two hours saying nothing, haven't you mediated long enough? She seemed anxious or worried about something, she told me, I just know we need to go!

Jules implied I have an idea lets go through the river of stone, let's head to the walking stone where it swings and overshadows the movement that flies alone, so we may cross over the river that laughs at fools!

Ada thought, "We won't be the fools, will we?"

While approaching this rocky overpass, the stones on the side banks were talking to each other while taking themselves a bath. As the water splashed and the winds slashed making things move about with strange sounds, we were crossing the crooked path of haste!

We found ourselves in the middle of the bridge of rock where it was swaying and bouncing around from side to side, raising its voice. It was shouting out, "Hurry, hurry, and hang on while there's still time!"

The creaks and crackling of popping rocks had us wondering if the bridge will hold up long enough to get us over to the other side without falling! Frighten by lack of hope with doubts has put both Ada and I in an unusual predicament, relying on the sympathy and relationship of a stone.

As we made it to the end of the other side, we looked back and saw a smile on the bridge of stone showing its natural harmony.

What was surprising, when looking back the bridge of stone with all its chilling agitation, was seemingly calm. Jules glanced at Ada, and she thought the bridge was resting easy for the next encroachment upon his path. Jules with astonishment was completely amazed. He thought maybe he doesn't want anybody on his back. Ada said, "Yeah, that's an easy way to put it."

As we were proceeding down the trail and up the hill, a path opened allowing the clearance that went under our feet to unfold, giving it some accessibility so it may breathe on its own again.

Slopes were dancing with the swinging curves; it happened to catch our eyes by surprise. It also prevented yourselves from slipping into and around corners!

When we looked up in the sky, it was shaken with noises that were running across the horizon with shouts as it was flying with the winds of time. it was gliding along a space not yet found! Ada and Jules were stunned watching and hearing echoes blaring along the clouds that were rushing by.

We were listening to the exotic sounds that were visiting us while seeking a path. Jules said to Ada, "There sure were some unusual occurrences that has taken place that put us into unexpected situations that got us caught inside the unknown."

Ada agreed, "Where did the exaggeration of this nightmare come from?"

Hearing the thoughts that we heard has persuaded our minds into asking yourselves, "Where does the harsh blare preside itself?"

The spin that shook us for a ride seemed to guide the twist that put us in a suspenseful daze! This happened to entangle our imagination that we've been trying to get past.

Ada asked, "Will this loosen the chains that have been holding us in a subliminal condition? Or will we have to take another ride on the Ferris wheel with lady luck?"

Jules smiled and said, "Where do we go from here, Ada?"

Standing on the Edge of Time

An appearance of a winnowing ripple, waving within a shivery ray, sparks a reflection outlining a portrait of mystery. This glow of sharpness brings a sudden brightness to flow along the valleys and mountaintops, "searching for a place to go."

Surrounded by treasures of brilliant alluring colors, the beauty of its fascination when looked upon dazzles the imagination. This peculiar glossiness you sense when viewing across the shiny sky engages a strange unlimited length that stretches "past a time not known."

Observing the quaintness of this pleasing sight brought a mystic fondness that took you beyond the clouds of rain.

This enchanting marvel guiding its way, traveling with speed you could not see, had you blinking when it went by with a "swooshing sound," and you heard the wind whispering while it passed you by!

The whisper spoke of a place not yet found but said, "Watch out, you've been standing on a cliff of make believe. If you were to fall, that will allow the darkness below to swallow you up without any chance of coming back."

This far distance that overextends an arm's reach had us removed from space, and we found ourselves coming from "another time!" Should we open our vision to notice the end may be near or have we been walking in a nightmare?

Standing in the middle of a lonely shadow. this frown upon his face showed a gloom when he discovered they were being led in the wrong direction. Eventually they found themselves on a brink of a steep mountain glancing down in a dark hole, allowing an extremity of wonderment to tremble from fear of a vertigo! When it shows the season, ride the wind before it's too late.

This swirling motion had you spinning while flying with the breeze that sent you sweeping alongside the oceanfront to see the waves crashing against the shores of rocks.

As the hidden undercurrent kept tumbling "around and around," water began to spin with us, and there seemed to be a connection.

While we floated above the surface, we were watching ourselves turning in opposite directions.

Persuasion of the splashing glitter had us follow the path it was taking, traveling underwater, listening to the sounds of overtones, whistling a harmony had you singing songs with the ocean.

The rushing turbulence had you blowing bubbles of air out as the breath of life took you riding with the tides. This whirling motion while crossing the sea of glass allowed you to sail, watching the brightness of splendor going past the "edge of time."

Bewildered by the array of its beauty left you speechless as this glowing exposure had your mind entangled, trying to acknowledge the source of this exquisite apostrophe!

Would the providence of a beginning initiate an introduction of its existence or have the ordinance been exhausted?

At what point have you notice it's not the same? As you're looking in front and what you see is yourselves going delirious, and you noticed, I'm all torn down, "but I'm standing up tall," but my back is flat on the ground! Waiting for your eyes, they slowly open to see if the unseen has been escorting your optical illusion.

There may be a devious restraint to hold us back, not knowing what to expect, that keeps us all in chains!

Who will set us free from the delusions that seem to be walking beside me while crossing the bridge of sigh? Standing on a mountain of dreams, the echoes of laughing rain has you puzzled. Where did the smiles come from?

A significant lover approached with a quarter moon smile, "eyes sparkling" as if a star was gazing in the winds of chime, bells ringing as she walked by, hands stretching to reach the sky, followed by tears burning way down in my heart!

An expression of a delirious fantasy was painted on my face. When we saw her flying to the clouds above, she had disappeared before our very sight!

When we turned to look behind, there was a door standing in the middle of the road, and as we came by, we went through it. As we turned back around, the door was gone. A small window was in its place!

As the window opened, a windy sensation passed by our ears when we thought, "Did we hear our calling?"

They were asking to come over to the other shore, so we may begin the next trip to a land "that shows time."

With the countless spectrums floating in the shiny air, the dazzling colors seem to change as you were running inside the circling orbit, "waiting for an asteroid" to come by, "so you may catch a ride on a star."

This motion sent you "round and round the sun," looking for a place to be dropped off. When the fascination led you flying over the ends of the world, you started noticing the seasons of nature with different forms along the way.

This spectacular metamorphose suggests a startling change, produced if by magic the action needed, "to enter into a future time." While sitting on the ridge farthest from the middle, an array of movements flinching along the clouds were performing a ritual dance!

As flashes of light jumping from one end to another had you holding onto the ledge, "fear put a frightening edge on your face!" You were afraid to glance down; there was no sight but darkness of blackness below.

The suspense was overwhelming, causing you to lose control of your natural sight. As forms of different conjectures entered inside your head wondering with uncertainty, "Will we be all right?"

Upon floating along and downward in the air, a dreamy sensation of wings flapped and glided me "to the edge of time!"

Standing on a cliff of no time revealed a space you couldn't walk on, and the brightness that took you there left you speechless.

This shiny radiance while crossing a path found its way along a beaming light, not understanding how it was touching the moon that had once disappeared.

The covering of the moon was enticing like a suspicious picture in a frame, not knowing what may come forth when unveiled.

While walking on a foggy mist of smoke, sloshes of splashing were heard, and the sounds seemed to be coming amongst the top half of the clouds.

After glancing above my head, a movement was flowing back and forth which put us in a state of disbelief. While focusing closely, we saw the seas they've been over our head. This had me curious, and how did the suspension keep them afloat?

How has a glossy greenish-blue liquid rising and guiding itself along the heights in its dimension sway a belief or two?

The formation along this gritty land, we could pick this up in my hands. This wonderful dryness was pleasing, extending myself to relax from the events that we saw from yesterdays.

As the storm's victorious triumph pounded, the surface made one have to escape a possible disaster. The translucent of a celestial object gave me a ride, adjoining a way through the luminous stars to a point of safety.

The guidance of the flight accommodated me so it would bring me back to a place of my desire.

An undecided choice on my behalf couldn't tell if one place was better than another.

I asked, "Is there no one who could choose for me because I don't know?"

They said, "There is one who knows a specific purpose that you truly admire."

I asked, "Who is that?"

"We will let you know when the time is right."